HUNTERSFORD LEIGH

Judge and Jury

SARA CLARIDGE

Chapter One

The mist swirled around Grace's feet as they pummelled the tarmac. She turned left off the village road and braced herself for the ache she was about to feel in her inner thighs as she jogged up the steep incline of the moor road.

She breathed deeply through the burn and welcomed the stretch of her muscles after the long flight halfway across the world. Already the heat of the Australian summer she'd left behind was a distant memory.

The mist grew thicker. Rising up in front of her as she left the warmth of the village behind her. She hadn't bothered with a headlamp. It reflected too much light against the dense air, making it harder to see.

She missed this. Up on the moor, the fog dampened the night's sounds to an eerie type of silence she'd never heard anywhere else in the world, but in Dartmoor. No other noise intruded on her thoughts, except for the metronomic pounding of her feet.

Not that she wanted to think at this moment.

She'd slept fitfully on the flight. Every time she closed her eyes she was transported to happier times. Her mother in the front garden, waiting for Grace to take the shortcut across the fields on her way home from school.

The garden had been her mother's pride and joy. The scent of lavender flowing through the windows on warm evenings was still as vivid in Grace's mind today as it had been when she was ten years old.

But then one day there was no one waiting for her. The cottage didn't smell of herbs and home cooking, but of hospitals and morphine. Grace blinked back the tears, and used the ball of her hand to swipe away the one that escaped. She picked up the pace. Outrunning bad memories was what she did best.

A dark shape appeared in front of her and she cried out involuntarily as a solid wall of muscle stopped her dead. Warm hands clamped around her upper arms, and a frisson of fear shuddered down her spine.

She'd been so deep in thought running up the road she'd stopped being aware of her surroundings. A foolish mistake and one she'd only made because she was still imagining the safe village she left behind twelve years ago.

There was much to fear in Huntersford Leigh, but being attacked wasn't one of them. Not in the dead of winter when all the tourists had gone, anyway. It hadn't occurred to her to bring protection.

She lifted her knee, hoping to connect with something vital, but she was trapped hard against the man's body.

"Grace? It's me."

The voice was low, soothing, possibly friendly. Her fear dropped a notch and she looked up from the hard chest she was currently pinned against, past the unyielding line of his jaw, until she focused on sharp eyes that missed nothing. The deep voice wasn't familiar, but the intense gaze staring down at her was unmistakable.

"Jesus, Dev. You scared the living daylights out of me."

His stance had an edge of menace that hadn't been there when they were young. Instinctively, she took a step back, forcing him to release his grip.

"Sorry. I heard someone running up the road—"

"What? So you thought you'd jump out and surprise them?" She forced her words out in between gasping breaths. Running up the hill and his surprise entrance had taken a toll on her equilibrium.

Normally she'd have kept her annoyance in check, but her heart was still in her throat from the fight or flight instinct he'd aroused. It didn't help that he looked like he'd barely be breaking into a sweat if their roles were reversed.

"I was concerned someone was in trouble. Who goes running on the moor in this weather?" His steely stare gave nothing away, but his sardonic tone made her see red.

"Clearly I was making my way back to the cottage."

His expression softened. "I'm sorry. I can hardly believe it."

No. Neither could she. She'd been reeling ever since the police had phoned a few days before. "Thanks."

She drew in a deep breath and released it slowly. The mist had thinned a little and a large four by four parked to one side of the road came into view. It was only then she realised she was standing right beside the cottage.

A tightness settled in her shoulders. She'd been away too long. In the past, it had never mattered how thick the fog whirled around her, she'd always known the exact location of her house. "Shit. If you hadn't had stopped me, I'd have continued up the road at least another quarter of a mile."

His lips rose in a faint smile, but it didn't reach his eyes. "Can we go inside for a minute?"

Grace wavered between answering him honestly and being polite. Travelling for the last twenty-four hours had wiped her out. She'd only gone for a run in the hope that releasing some tension would help her sleep. Reminiscing over old times wasn't high on her list of priorities.

For a moment she thought about denying his request, but Devlin would think it strange and only ask more questions. The quickest way to get rid of him would be to let him in and find out what he wanted.

"Sure." Leading the way down the garden path to the front door, she unzipped her pocket and dug out the key.

"You found it okay?"

Grace grimaced. She'd forgotten what it was like to live in a small community where everyone knew each other's business.

"It was right where Mrs Hargreaves said it would be." Under a flowerpot beside the door, as if that wouldn't be the first place even the worst burglar in the world would look. Still, she shouldn't complain. Mrs Hargreaves always had an idealistic view of the tourists that flocked to Dartmoor in the summer.

Stepping over the threshold, Grace held the door open for Devlin to follow her inside. His vast framed filled the tiny hallway in a way it had never done when they were teenagers.

This afternoon, when she'd first come in, it was like walking into a time warp. Not much had changed since she left for university. Even the flowery wallpaper was just as her mother had hung it. Although now it was faded in places where the sun shone through the kitchen, and the edges a little frayed here and there. But the sight of it still filled her with the love and happiness she'd felt as a child.

The only new thing in the hallway was the luggage she hadn't carried upstairs yet.

Devlin's gaze alighted on it and he looked back at her, his eyebrows raised. "I guess travelling on commercial airlines is a lot rougher than I remember."

"It's my camera gear. I can never guarantee how it's treated once it's out of my sight. The strengthened cases protect the lenses from almost anything."

She'd learnt that the hard way.

He made a move towards it. "Do you need a hand shifting it?"

"No thanks."

He stopped and frowned. "It looks heavy."

"It is, but I'm used to it."

Those few boxes were her life. They'd been everywhere with her, from the rainforests of Suriname in search of a rare frog to the base camp of Everest where her photos of the elusive snow leopard ended up winning her a coveted award.

She wasn't ready to take the equipment up to her old room just yet. At least here on the hallway floor it felt as if she could still flee at a moment's notice. Before the truth escaped.

The grandfather clock ticked steadily behind her. The silence in their conversation stretched out uncomfortably. Did Dad still wind it on a Sunday? She'd have to remember to do so soon, before it stopped.

Devlin's stance shifted as he switched his weight from one leg to the other. It didn't strike her as an impatient move. But one to make himself more comfortable.

Well, he was the one hanging around. At this rate she was never going to get rid of him. "Why did you come, Dev? I don't believe you're the welcoming committee."

The glint in his eyes confirmed he at least still had his sense of humour.

"Mum. She saw the light on and wanted me to check on my way home."

"You still live with your parents?"

His brow drew down. "What? No. I haven't lived at home since I was seventeen."

Of course. She remembered the day he left. In the throng of people that had gathered to wish him well, he'd hugged her and said he'd miss their daily walks. She doubted he remembered them now.

"I'm the other side of the village." He tipped his head to indicate across the river. "Dad has a cold and Mum didn't want to send him out in this weather."

Grace shook her head and let out a sigh. Mrs Judge had been looking out for her from the day her mum got sick.

"Besides, she knows I pass the moor road on my way back from Exeter, so it was no trouble."

Maybe letting Devlin come in was a mistake. She wasn't normally so ungrateful for people's kindness. But she was cranky and out of sorts. The adrenalin that had been pumping round her body was fading and in its place was a bone-deep tiredness. Not from the jet lag. She was used to that. But from the heartache of coming home.

Giving herself a mental shake, Grace forced herself to smile. "Tell her thank you, and I'll go up and see her tomorrow."

She thought that would appease Devlin and he'd be on his way, but he seemed to be hovering by the door, with something on his mind. It wasn't like him to be shy about saying what he thought. It was one of the things she'd admired most about him when her mum died.

Everyone else seemed to walk over eggshells unsure how to act or what to say. But Devlin treated her as if her world hadn't just fallen apart. That day he'd shown up at the door on her first day at senior school insisting that she walk with him to the bus stop had been a turning point for her.

He probably did it under duress from his mother, but those walks, as brief as they were, rescued her from the grief that overshadowed every other part of her life.

The clock struck nine, and she yawned, hoping that Dev would get the hint. Not that she was likely to sleep for several hours yet, no matter how tired she felt.

Finally, he opened the door and made a move to leave. At the last moment he turned. The look of disappointment in his eyes stilled her heart.

"He missed you, you know. You should have come back sooner."

Her throat constricted as the bitter lump of betrayal wedged itself in her chest. Sod being polite. Willing her hand not to shake with the anger that had spiked along with her blood pressure, she grabbed the handle out of his grasp, yanked the door open wider, and pushed him back outside.

CHAPTER TWO

The cold night air hit Devlin like a bucket of ice water as Grace thrust him over the threshold. She'd caught him off guard with the speed of her reaction to his words, her slight form belaying a deeper strength.

He straightened up and met her piercing stare.

"Go home, Devlin."

He should heed her curt tone and return another day. But he couldn't leave yet. Not without telling her. As the door began to close, he stepped forward, grasping the edge of it with his hand.

"Wait. Give me a minute."

She let out a sigh. "Why? So you can berate me again for something you know nothing about?"

"But I do, that's the point."

Her brow creased in a frown. "You haven't seen me in years. You weren't even here for the last two I spent in the village. How can you possibly know anything about my relationship with my father?"

He raked a hand through his hair. Hell. In his mind, this conversation had been so much easier. "When I got back from Iraq, we talked. A lot."

She blinked, slowly, as if she was taking it all in, but her expression remained blank.

He couldn't understand why she was so indifferent to her father's death. "Your dad was really proud of everything you'd achieved. He'd always have a clip from a magazine article or something you sent him in an email to show anyone that cared to look."

"Well, there's your proof. I wasn't the bad daughter you make me out to be."

Devlin sighed. In the darkness of the night, with only the low glow from the lamp in the hallway behind her, Grace's face was in the shadows. But he could still see those alluring hazel eyes shuttering her true emotions. Just as they'd done when they were kids.

Maybe he was wrong. Maybe she did care. He, more than anyone, should understand how it was easier to keep the pain hidden deep inside. "I didn't say you were bad. I just meant he missed you. Christ, Grace. You didn't even come back for a visit."

Her jaw tightened a fraction, and the pressure of the door closing increased beneath his hand. He put his foot against the base of it for insurance. She wasn't going to take him by surprise again.

"I'm not having this discussion, Devlin. Just because you had *long conversations* with my father, it doesn't give you the right to interfere in my life."

He swallowed hard. Her words were closer to the truth than she realised. When he'd first agreed to Geoff's request, he'd been curious as to how Grace might react. But ever since he heard the news of her father's death, he'd been dreading this confrontation.

He needed to get this out before the conversation spiralled downwards even further. "There's something else."

She leaned into the door, defeated. "Can't it wait? I'm tired and this has been a long few days."

"No." Devlin swore under his breath and prayed that Geoff had known what he was doing. "How much do you know about your father's will?"

Her eyes narrowed. "Nothing. I wasn't even sure he'd made one."

Fuck. He'd made one all right. "It's with a solicitor based over in Okehampton."

"Okay. Thanks for letting me know. Night, Dev. I'll see you around."

She tried to close the door again, and he flattened his hand against it.

"Hold on. That's not all."

Her brows raised in silent question.

"He made me the executor."

"The solicitor?"

"No. Your dad."

Her lips pursed as she digested the information. After a moment, she lifted her chin and met his gaze. He was taken right back to when they'd last seen each other all those years ago. Acceptance. Before she even knew what he was about to tell her, it was acceptance of her fate. As if fighting for something wouldn't make a difference to the end result, so there was no point in trying.

"He's left you something?"

"No." He ran a hand through his hair as her meaning struck home. "Christ, no! It's all yours. But you need to speak to the solicitor." He took a deep breath. "There are...conditions."

Impatience flitted through her eyes. He couldn't determine if it was aimed at him or her father.

"What are you not saying, Dev?"

"It's better the solicitor explains it. I'll set up a meeting for us."

Her posture stiffened against the door at his use of the word *us*.

"I'm sorry, Grace. I don't mean to obfuscate, but when you see the will, you'll understand."

She threw her hand up in front of him. "Why can't you just tell me?"

He was too scared. Did that make him a wuss? Probably. But he was man enough to admit it. "It's complicated."

"He was a simple man." She gestured to the cottage that hadn't changed in years. "A clean house, food on the table, and a little money for a rainy day was all that mattered."

He reached out and ran the back of his finger across her cheek. "Who loved you very much."

Grace turned her face away from his touch. "So much so that he put conditions on what he left me."

Devlin frowned. "And what conditions did you make when he was alive?"

Her eyes widened. The hurt in them was unmistakable. Caught in the memories of the past, he'd spoken without thinking. He took a step back in retreat.

"Goodnight, Devlin. Make the appointment. Just make it soon. I'm not planning on hanging around."

Before he could say that was exactly what she would be doing, Grace closed the door.

He stood there for a moment. How had he managed to so spectacularly fuck up something that should have been straightforward? Shaking his head at his own ineptitude, he headed back towards his car.

He was nearly at the end of the path when he heard it. A sob from behind the door Grace had just closed. Guilt twisted in his gut. He'd been so busy thinking about how much Geoff had missed Grace, he hadn't really thought about what it must be like for her. To finally come back only to find her home a hollow shell of what it was before.

Cursing himself, he walked back to the door. "I'm sorry, Grace."

A muffled cry came from somewhere near the letter box. He pictured her huddled on the floor, sunk against the door, and closed his eyes. Why hadn't he kept his mouth shut? He'd promised her father he'd look out for her, and the first time he tried, he made her cry.

He cleared his throat and made a conscious effort to keep his voice calm. "Please open the door."

"Go away."

"Not until I know you're okay."

A sarcastic snort reached his ears. "I'm fine. Never better."

The mist swirled around him as he stood on the step, unsure of what to do next. At least it sounded like she'd stopped crying.

"Grace?"

"Just leave me alone, Dev. You've done enough tonight."

He briefly closed his eyes and took a deep breath, before marching back to his car, calling himself all kinds of a fool every step of the way.

Grace hiccuped as she swiped the tears from her eyes.

Bastard. What gave him the right to criticise her? What did he know? He got out. Escaped to the army and never looked back.

She inhaled deeply and then slowly released her breath. The anger felt good. Better than the numbness she'd felt since the police had called. Not that she'd ever give Devlin the satisfaction of knowing he'd helped bring her out of the mental fog she'd been in.

Ever since she'd answered the policeman's tentative "Miss Vaughan?" she'd been wavering between sadness, regret, and dread.

If it wasn't for the fact that despite their differences, she still loved her father, she would never have come back to Huntersford Leigh. It wasn't as if she or the village had missed each other in the twelve years she'd been gone.

But she couldn't let a stranger organise her father's funeral, or pay someone to go through the house and clear it out. So here she was. Trapped for the next couple of weeks between gossiping villagers and so-called friends that asked too many questions.

Taking a tissue from her pocket, Grace blew her nose and wiped her face.

Give Devlin his due. He'd sounded genuinely regretful as he spoke to her through the door. But she'd waited until she heard the garden gate close, before giving in again to the sobs that racked her body.

Her throat started to tighten again. She forced the emotion down and latched back onto the anger.

And what the fuck was he getting at about Dad's will? Why her dad thought it needed Dev as an executor was beyond her. She'd meant it earlier when she said her dad was a simple man. There was the house, sure, but probably not much would be left after the bank was paid what was owed to them.

Raising her chin, Grace glanced through to the living room and caught sight of her mum's favourite vase on the mantelpiece. Another tear escaped her eyes and she brushed it aside. All she needed was a few keepsakes to remember the happier days.

Although quite what she'd do with them, she wasn't sure. Personal belongings didn't fit into her nomadic lifestyle. Perhaps she'd finally have to get a storage unit. She tilted her head back against the door. Just one more problem to solve.

Closing her eyes to blot out the memories that surrounded her, she let out a shuddering breath. She'd only been back a day and already she was regretting it.

Chapter Three

Devlin woke with a start, the thump of his heart vibrating harder than a Chinook's rotating blades.

He threw off the sheet that covered him and drew in a deep breath. The cool air washed over his sweat-drenched body and chased the nightmare away.

It was just a dream. He closed his eyes again. The reality had been so much worse.

He gave himself a moment to recover before glancing at the bedside clock. Five fifteen. His alarm was about to go off. Might as well get up. Sleep was never going to come now.

Swinging his legs over the side of the bed, he stood up slowly, stretching his leg muscles. Days like this, he was careful not to demand too much from his body until he'd completed his warm-up exercises.

He couldn't figure it out, but he'd swear there was a correlation between the nightmares and the functioning of his legs.

All part of the healing process, according to the surgeon, but after six months, he was starting to think he was just going to have to get used to it. Atonement for his mistake.

He pulled on some running gear and threw a change of clothes into his bag. An hour in the gym before work would help ease his legs and his stress.

Easing out of the drive, Devlin flicked on the car radio and soft rock spilled out of the speakers. One thing about not being able to sleep, at least the roads were clear this time of day. It wasn't long before he left the dark lanes behind and picked up the main road to Exeter.

On the outskirts of town, he turned off and made his way to Agema. Swiping his card at the secure entrance of the defence contractor, he parked in his normal spot underground, and then took the lift to the company gym.

When the doors opened, he walked over to where Jamie was on the treadmills, greeting several colleagues on the way. Placing his sports bag down by a nearby bench, he gave his friend a once-over. "Didn't expect to see you here."

Jamie wiped the sweat away from his face with a towel hanging over the handrail. "Landed this morning. I needed to work off some of the tension. What's your excuse?"

Devlin set the treadmill next to him at an easy pace. "Couldn't sleep."

He didn't need to explain further. Jamie had been a regular visitor while Devlin was recovering. Though they'd taken separate paths in the military, on the rare occasions their paths crossed, they'd always worked well together. And those life threatening situations solidified their childhood friendship even more.

When the army discharged Devlin on medical grounds, Jamie had convinced him that he'd be better off at Agema. More pay, less red tape. He wasn't convinced about the bureaucracy, and shareholders had their own agenda, just like the army. But he conceded that without Jamie's intervention, he'd have been lost back in the real world with too much time on his hands.

All he needed to do now was get back to full fitness and back out in the field. Stuck behind a desk, there was too much damn time to think about what he should have done differently.

Jamie pulled out his ear buds and let them dangle in front of him. "I hear Grace is back."

Devlin groaned inwardly. The village rumour mill was in full force. He'd been working in intelligence for years, but it always amazed him the speed with which news spread through Huntersford. "Yeah. I dropped by last night."

"Really? You didn't waste much time."

Devlin gave his friend a sideways glare. "Mum rang me on the way home. She saw a light and wanted me to check."

Jamie grinned. "Mummy's boy. Wasn't it enough that she made you walk Grace to the school bus every day?"

A small spike of ire hit Devlin in defence of Grace. "Mum only asked me to do it the once. It was her first day at senior school, you jerk."

Jamie raised an eyebrow. "So, why did you continue?"

"I was going in that direction, anyway." Devlin hit the button on the treadmill with his finger and sped up. Normally, he enjoyed the easy banter with Jamie. They'd been trading barbs since kindergarten, but today he was unsettled. Maybe it was the nightmare. Or maybe it was the seeing the pain he'd caused Grace, knowing there was more to come.

"Has she changed much?"

He thought back to the way she'd looked last night in the dim light of the hall. Her dark hair curling around her shoulders, the flecks of gold in her hazel eyes emphasised by the colour of her tanned skin.

Devlin glanced over at Jamie, who was still waiting for him to answer. "A bit. Still as smart as a whip. But she's lost that air of fragility."

There was a steely strength in her as she threw him out of the house last night. An assertiveness that hadn't been there when they were young.

"Maybe I should go say hello."

"Jesus, Jamie. She's just lost her dad. She doesn't need to be fending you off."

Jamie's smirk returned and Devlin knew his friend hadn't missed the growl in his tone.

"No. She's too busy dealing with you."

"Fuck off."

In his peripheral vision, he could see Jamie's smile widen. Devlin hit the incline button and adjusted to the harder pace. Jamie might be one of his oldest friends, but sometimes that was a curse, not a blessing.

He frowned as he thought about Jamie's accusation. Truth be told, he'd been trying hard not to think about Grace. It was going to be difficult enough around her over the next few days, without letting the instant attraction he'd felt take hold. Especially once she found out the details of the will.

They continued in silence, focusing on their routines until Jamie pressed a button on the console and his machine started to slow.

"See you later?"

"Yeah. I think we've got a call with the US at ten."

"Okay. We'll do it in your office, it's quieter. I'll bring coffee and cupcakes."

Devlin's mouth rose in a half smile and he shook his head at his friend's lost cause. "It doesn't matter how many you buy, she's never going to give in and agree to go on a date with you."

"I can only ask."

"Yeah. But every day is getting stalkerish."

"Says the guy that turns up the first night the girl next door comes home."

If he hadn't been worried that his legs might fail him after this morning's nightmare, he'd have let go of the treadmill handrail and flipped Jamie his middle finger.

Grace woke the next morning to a sense of surreality. Dad hadn't changed a thing over the years. Teenage idols from over a decade ago still looked down on her from the posters stuck to the wall, while running medals and trophies lined the shelves instead of books.

She squinted at the teal patchwork curtains and couldn't help but smile. Maybe she was as bad as Dad. When she'd re-decorated her room as a teenager, she'd refused his offer to pay for new curtains because she could still remember Mum taking her to Launceston to buy them originally. She just didn't remember the light shining through them quite so brightly.

Not setting an alarm seemed sensible last night, but now she was seriously regretting it. The glare of the sun was high for January, so she must have slept late. Rolling over in the bed, she grabbed her phone from the nightstand. Half-past nine. Shit.

She got out of bed and dressed in the jeans, t-shirt, and sweatshirt she'd worn last night after her shower. Maybe once she'd finished with the police later today, she'd have time to buy some warmer clothes.

The bang of the knocker on the front door made her jump. So much for her hope of escaping Huntersford Leigh without anyone realising she'd come back. Although, given her father's car crash had made the local news that wasn't a very realistic expectation.

Running down the stairs to answer the door, she paused briefly at the bottom and glanced at herself in the hall mirror to check she was presentable.

"It's only me, Grace," a voice called out.

Devlin's mother. The sound of the familiar voice lifted some of her depression. Reaching to unlatch the lock, she barely had a chance to open the door fully before she was grasped in a big hug that brought tears to her eyes and forced her to choke down the unexpected emotion.

"You poor thing. I can't believe it." Mrs Judge hoisted her back a fraction, not letting go of her shoulders. "You've grown too thin. All those gruelling photo trips your dad was always telling us about, I expect."

Grace sniffed back the tears and smiled. She was unsure whether she was expected to answer and to which statement. Her gaze dropped to the bag of groceries on the step.

Dev's mum gave a sheepish smile. "I wasn't sure if you had time yesterday to stop off at the shops, so I brought you a few essentials to keep you going."

"Aww, Mrs Judge, that's so nice of you, but you didn't have to."

"I wanted to. And I think we're probably past the Mrs Judge stage, don't you? Call me Anna." She picked up the bag and Grace stepped aside before following her into the kitchen.

"You'll stay for a cuppa, won't you, Anna?"

"Wild horses wouldn't stop me."

Grace filled the kettle as Anna put the groceries away, refusing her offer to pay for them. From the way she bustled around the kitchen, Grace could tell she must have still looked after her dad, just as she kept an eye on the pair of them after Mum died.

There was a kind of normalcy about it that soothed her. As if her father would walk through the back door at any moment, forgetting as always to take off his muddy boots.

She reached for the milk carton Anna had set beside her and cried out as she knocked it to the floor. "Damn. Sorry Anna, all your hard work undone in a moment of my clumsiness."

Anna reached for the carton as Grace grabbed a cloth to mop up the milk that had spilled. "It's okay, there's still plenty there for our tea. I expect you're just tired from all that travelling. I can fetch you another one from the house."

"No, don't bother. You've already done so much. I'm going out later to Exeter. I can pick one up then."

"If you're sure. I don't mind, I always have plenty."

"Please, Anna, don't worry. I'll start to feel guilty." Placing the two mugs of tea on the small kitchen table, Grace took the chair she'd always sat in since she grew out of her highchair.

Anna sat down opposite and reached across to squeeze Grace's hand. "We're all so sorry about your dad."

"Thanks. Do you know what happened? All I heard from the police was that there had been a road accident. I need to go and see them later on today."

"Down the old Leigh road, was all I heard. Went off the road and into a tree." Her face creased into a wince as if she hated to be the deliverer of more distress in an already painful situation.

"It's all so hard to take in. I wonder where he was going?"

Anna gave a small shake of her head. "Not sure. I thought the same thing."

Grace sighed and stared into her mug. "I'll guess we'll never know now."

"Do you want Mick to go with you to the police?"

She lifted her head and met Anna's concerned look. "No. I'm fine. Besides, Devlin said he wasn't well."

"Listen to me." Anna shook her head as she berated herself. "Offering help to the girl that takes on lions and tigers."

Grace laughed. It felt good to have a lighter moment. "You make me sound like I work in the circus, not photography. It was koalas, anyway. Not nearly as dangerous."

"Devlin could take you? He's in Exeter anyway. I'm sure he could spare you some time. Shall I call him?" Anna reached for her bag, no doubt to find her mobile.

"No. Please, don't worry. It's no problem." She'd been about to say that she'd already agreed to meet the police at the mortuary to identify the body, but thankfully she realised just in time that Anna would never let her do that alone. So she kept quiet.

Neither would Dev, a voice inside of her confirmed. Despite his harsh words yesterday. But neither of them understood. They only saw what her father wanted them to see, just as it had been growing up. She studied Anna for a moment. No. Maybe Anna understood more than her younger self realised.

But who was she to turn everything on its head now? And what did it matter if Devlin thought her selfish? She'd be gone in a few weeks. Three max, she'd estimated. With no links to Huntersford, she'd soon be forgotten. A ghost of the past. No different to Idonea. *Except, of course, that the ancient warrior wouldn't have run away.*

Anna placed her hand over Grace's again, pulling her back to the present. "If you're sure."

Now would be the perfect opportunity to see if Anna knew anything about her father's will. "Yes. Thank you. Devlin's already offered to sort out a meeting with Dad's solicitor. I don't want to trouble him any more than necessary."

"Oh that's good," Anna beamed. "He's such a thoughtful boy."

An image of Devlin standing in the hall flashed into her mind. He didn't seem much of a boy last night. Not how she remembered him, anyway. All muscle and coiled tension, ready to rake her over the coals for her perceived misdeeds.

But as the conversation progressed, it didn't take long for Grace to realise Anna knew even less than her about the will. She hadn't even known that her son was the executor. Was that because Devlin had been asked not to say anything, or was he respecting her privacy, despite the fact he had no problem telling her his view on the situation?

Grace frowned as a final thought flickered into her mind. Or were the conditions so weird he didn't want anyone finding out?

Anna cleared her throat and Grace gave her an apologetic smile. "Sorry, my mind wandered."

"Don't worry, love. I understand." She gulped down the rest of her tea and stood. "Well, I'd better be off. Come up and see us in a day or so once you're settled." She held up a hand as Grace started to rise. "Don't get up. I'll see myself out."

"Okay. Tell Mick to get well soon and thank you again for the groceries. You're a lifesaver, as always."

"Oh, it's nothing. What's the point of living in a small community if you don't look after each other?" With that, she was through the door and on her way.

Grace sat back in her chair and folded her arms, Anna's parting comment whirling through her mind. She wasn't sure she shared Anna's idealistic view of the people of Huntersford Leigh.

Her gaze drifted to the flyer held onto the fridge door by a magnet, the bold text advertising the annual pub quiz at The Idonea Arms. She could just imagine the village gossip shared over a pint once the truth came out about her father.

Chapter Four

Walking back to his car after a client lunch in Exeter town centre, Devlin tensed as the soft curse reached his ears. He recognised that voice. Back-tracking his steps past the concrete column in the multi-storey car park, Grace came into view.

He'd already planned to stop by the house tonight on his way home and tell her he'd booked a meeting with the solicitor. Perhaps fate was lending him a helping hand. He'd been dreading facing her again after yesterday evening. Maybe this way he could get it over with sooner. Although, judging from her agitated state, perhaps now wasn't the best time.

She looked up as he approached, and a flicker of resignation flitted across her face. He guessed he was the last person she wanted to talk to right now.

"Hi. Is everything okay?"

As he drew closer, he could see her flushed cheeks and clenched jaw. What on earth had happened to get her so angry? At least he wasn't responsible for it this time.

She glanced down at the windscreen beside her. "I'd be just fine if someone would give me a break. Why can't people realise that I didn't deliberately place the car across two places? Everyone else parked badly."

Devlin regarded the cars parked precisely within the white markings on either side of her rental.

Grace raised her hands defensively as she caught his look. "Except, of course, now I look bad, because in the meantime all the other cars have left and sensible people have parked in their places."

Picking up a piece of cardboard wedged under the wiper, she threw it towards the front of the car, where it slumped skee-wiff against the concrete wall, FUCKING BITCH! emblazoned across it.

Now he understood her ire. He felt his own rising at the very sight of it. "How did they know you were a woman?"

She frowned as if she couldn't see the relevance to his question. "They didn't. Which just proves it was written by some wanker who presumes all women are bad drivers."

He couldn't fault her logic, but the note seemed a bit extreme for a shopping mall car park. And there was something about the way the capital letters looped together that made him think differently. But seeing the glint in Grace's look that dared him to challenge her opinion, he kept his thoughts to himself.

He'd spent so many years looking for hidden meanings, clues, and intelligence in the smallest, most insignificant piece of information that sometimes he forgot that in the civilian world, things were often exactly as they seemed.

She stomped to the back of the car, where she'd left a couple of clothes-store bags, and placed them in the boot before turning to face him, seemingly surprised he was still there. "What now?"

He shrugged. "I don't know. It seems like an odd time to go shopping." He regretted the words as soon as they'd left his mouth.

Frustrated at his own inability to think straight around Grace, he shoved his hands in his pockets and mentally cursed Geoff for making everything so freaking awkward. Then he let out a sigh for thinking ill of the dead.

She propped a hip against the car. "If you must know, I needed warm clothes. All I have is what was in my wardrobe for Australia and it's still summer there."

He pictured the cases in the hallway yesterday evening. He'd presumed she'd taken a bag with her clothes upstairs already, but maybe not. "You didn't stop by your place on the way down here to swap your clothes?"

She gave a slight shake of her head. "I don't have a place."

The information caught him by surprise. He'd always assumed she had a flat in London. "But where do you live in between assignments?"

Grace glared. Yeah, maybe he needed to improve his conversation technique and make it less of an interrogation.

"I'm normally exploring wherever I am. Making the most of the free flight that got me there."

At his continuing silence, she huffed out a sigh. "Seriously? With everything going on, your biggest question is why I'm buying clothes? If you must know, I've a few bits and pieces, but mostly I just buy clothes wherever I am and find a recycle bin or charity shop when I'm done with them. As you've already seen, I've enough luggage already, and it's cheaper than paying rent or a mortgage on somewhere just to keep a wardrobe when I'd never be there. Satisfied?"

Devlin tilted his head and frowned. "What do you use for an official address?"

Grace scowled at him. "Dad's house. He just messages me if a letter looks important." The glower slipped. "Or at least he used to."

Which reminded him of the solicitor's appointment.

Now some of the flush had gone from her initial anger at the note on her car, he could see she was pale beneath her tan. Dark shadows smudged the skin underneath her eyes. Had his harsh words last night put them there? Or had he just not noticed in the dimly lit hallway yesterday and his haste to tell her about the will?

He clenched his fist and tapped it on her car. "I'm sorry about yesterday, Grace. I should have chosen my words more carefully."

She gave him a frosty look, but stayed silent.

As apologies went, this wasn't great. He should probably just cut his losses and tell her now about the appointment. "I've booked a meeting for Monday with the solicitors."

She stiffened and mumbled her thanks.

"Did you want me to pick you up?"

"No, thanks. I'll meet you there. Text me the address." She rattled off her number and then paused. "Don't you want to write it down?"

"No. I've got it memorised. I'll send you a message later." He reached out to touch her arm. "Are you sure you're okay?"

Her lips rose a little. "I'm fine, Dev." She looked as if she was wrestling with herself about saying more. "I'm sorry too, for snapping at you. I had to identify the body today and I guess I'm still a little off kilter." She gestured back towards the cardboard notice. "And that didn't help either."

Hell. He'd done more than his fair share of that over the years. No wonder she looked pale. "I'm sorry, Grace. You should have said. I could have come with you."

He stilled under her sardonic stare. Yeah, he probably was the last person she'd have called this morning.

"Dad wouldn't have wanted people to see him that way." She slammed the boot shut.

"Was it bad?"

She took a deep breath and released it slowly. "They said the bruising was normal. Caused by the airbag deployment, and the force as his head hit the steering wheel."

Devlin frowned. "He wasn't wearing a seatbelt?"

Her gaze met his and for a fraction of a second, he glimpsed the pain there. He'd been wrong yesterday. She wasn't indifferent to her father's death.

"I presumed he was. I don't think they mentioned it. It doesn't matter, anyway. All the safety in the world isn't going to help if you wrap your car around a tree."

He caught the note of anger in her voice and understood. The senselessness of it. The overwhelming feeling of helplessness.

Grace blinked hard. "Despite all our differences over the years, it breaks my heart to think of him lying there alone on the Leigh road for several hours."

She didn't say, but he surmised she meant before succumbing to his injuries.

"Do they know what caused the accident?"

She shifted from one foot to the other. "They wanted to know if I had any idea where he was going."

The subtle change in her tone raised a red flag. She was avoiding answering. He forced himself not to immediately ask again. She might have been willing to appease him and answer his questions earlier, but he was certain that she would be harder to crack than some hardened insurgent if she didn't want him to know something.

He followed her lead. "It's an odd road for him to be on, I agree. I can't think of a single local that uses it, even in the off season. Unless he was taking some sort of shortcut over to the camp?"

"But why would he be going there? It's not exactly restful even when you guys aren't using it. Besides, I'm not even sure that's possible from that road."

His mouth quirked at *you guys*. He knew she meant the army, but working for Agema, it often felt like he hadn't left. Faces were the same. The intelligence briefings he gave were the same. Even the politics were the same. But now he was on the other side of the fence, with less government red tape and more freedom to work off his own initiative.

He tried another tack. "Did the police say why they thought he went off the road? It wasn't icy that night."

The lift across the car park pinged and Grace glanced over sharply, as if worried about being overheard. "They're not sure at this stage. Something about still finalising their report."

Another hedge. He pushed a little more. "Do you want me to see if I can find out any more information for you? I have some contacts I could ask."

The blood draining from her face was all he needed to see to confirm that she was hiding something.

"No. It's fine, thank you. They appear to be very thorough in their investigation."

Her hasty response made the back of his neck itch. Yep. So thorough they'd discovered something she didn't want to come to light.

"Well, if you're sure you're alright, I'll let you get going."

He stepped to one side as she got in and reversed out of the parking spot, then walked to his car. She was right. He might have had long chats with her father, but that didn't make him an expert on Geoff's relationship with his daughter.

He scrubbed a hand over his face. The whole thing didn't make sense. Why hadn't she been home in all this time?

As Grace walked into the corner shop on Huntersford Leigh's main street the next day, the chatter stopped abruptly.

Behind the counter, Mrs Cole began busily scanning the items in front of her.

"Don't stop on my account," Grace called out.

The three women gathered by the till glanced at each other, and realisation dawned on Grace. Obviously they'd been talking about her, or Dad. She bent her head as she walked over to the rack of magazines to prevent them from seeing the flush blooming on her cheeks.

"I'm sorry to hear about your father," Mrs Pritchett said across the aisles, and Mrs Davis murmured her agreement.

Grace drew in a breath and straightened her shoulders. Cursing herself for forgetting to pick up some milk on way home yesterday after the episode in the car park, she turned around to face the three sisters.

"Thank you." She tried to keep the curtness out of her tone, but was sure she'd failed.

"When's the funeral? Let me know and I can spread the word for you," said Mrs Pritchett.

Grace had no doubt the woman would take great delight, since she had always circulated most of the gossip. "There's no date yet. But it will be at the crematorium at Exeter."

The woman's brow arched a fraction in silent disapproval, and Grace could feel ire rise within her.

"Not at the church over at Chagford?" asked Mrs Cole.

"No. Dad wasn't much of a churchgoer." Especially after her mum died.

"Are you sure?" Mrs Pritchett's tone implied that Grace might be mistaken.

Of course she was bloody well sure.

Before she could form a response, Mrs Davis spoke up. "It's been a while since you've seen him, dear. I'm certain the vicar would be willing to talk with you."

Fucking hell. These three had been bad enough before, but she was damned if she'd let them start meddling in her life now. She opened her mouth to refute the claim, but realised just in time it would be futile. She'd only end up giving them more ammunition to feed the village rumour mill.

Instead, she gave the three women her sweetest smile. "Thank you for your concern, but I know Dad would be perfectly happy with the arrangements I'm making."

She walked over to the cooler cabinet and picked up a pint of milk. Bloody Devlin. If he hadn't riled her up again yesterday with all his questions, she would never have forgotten to pick up milk and wouldn't be here now, facing these three witches.

She stood in line behind witch number three. Despite having bagged up her shopping and paid her sister, Mrs Pritchett still stood by the till, clearly not wanting to miss any little bit of tittle-tattle she could use to fuel more gossip.

"What about flowers? I'm sure the ladies in the flower arranging society would welcome the opportunity to provide you with something special."

"No, thank you."

"They're very good. They did old Mrs Smith's flowers for her funeral. Looked spectacular, really nice."

"There won't be any flowers. Dad always said flowers looked their best where they grew. He thought cutting them to die in a vase was a waste of their beauty."

A searing pain of heartache seized her chest as she remembered the beautiful orchid a friend had sent to her mum when she was first ill. It stayed constantly in bloom for the few short months she lived. After that, her father never had flowers in the house again.

She tried to take a deep breath, but her throat was constricted with the tears she held back. The clash with these old battle axes was suffocating her. She desperately needed to get out of here before she lost it completely.

Her gaze slid to the shop counter. Mrs Cole still hadn't even started to ring up Mrs Davis' goods. "Sorry, could I squeeze in front of you? I've only a pint of milk and I'm in a bit of a hurry."

Mrs Davis stepped to one side. "Course, love. I've all the time in the world."

Grace wasn't sure if the woman was being sarcastic or not, but she didn't care. She just needed to get away. "Thanks." She handed the correct change to Mrs Cole and picked up her milk. "I'll be sure to let you know the date. See you around."

Tears stung the back of her eyes as she walked out of the shop. She'd been right all along. Coming back was a huge mistake.

If she was ever going to breathe freely again, she needed to go to the one place that had always been her sanctuary.

Chapter Five

Devlin looked up as Jamie leant against the jamb of his office door.

"Have you got a minute?"

Tapping the computer screen, Devlin shut down the report he'd been reading. "Sure. Take a seat."

Jamie slumped into the chair in front of Devlin's desk. "I spoke to Geordie earlier."

His friend paused, obviously trying to gauge Devlin's reaction. In the early days after the explosion, the mention of one of his old teammates would have sent Devlin spiralling into introspection.

But he'd quickly realised the best way to honour the dead was to continue working to keep others safe. Everyone said there was no way he could have known that an informant they'd relied on for years had suddenly had his family taken hostage, and would walk them into a trap. Maybe they were right. Maybe they weren't.

Still wouldn't bring Ronnie back from the dead.

He met Jamie's concerned stare. "Yeah? What did he have to say?"

"Not much, just the usual shit. He said he was concerned about Ella."

A heavy weight hit the pit of Devlin's stomach. There was always more than one victim. Ella had taken the news of Ronnie's death hard.

She still blamed Devlin, as much as he did himself, for the loss of her wife. "What's wrong?"

"He says it's like she's strung out on meds again. Everything looks normal, but there's a vibe he can't place. She's put away all the photos of Ronnie, but he said her gaze is constantly going to where they should be."

Devlin rested his elbows on the table, steepled his fingers, and pressed his mouth against them. "Do you think I should go see her?"

Jamie shrugged. "I don't know. Damned if you do, damned if you don't."

Devlin gave a faint smile, acknowledging the truth in those words. The last time he tried to talk to Ella, she'd started throwing things at him, forcing him to back out the house in full retreat. But if he didn't check on her, then he'd be letting one of his team down. Even if Ronnie wasn't here to know it, Devlin would.

"Dev?"

He raised his gaze to Jamie's.

"If you decide to go, take someone with you this time. Geordie said he'd be up for the job."

He sighed and sat back. "Yeah. Good advice."

He and Geordie had both served with Ronnie, but Geordie got out and joined Agema nine months before he did.

Jamie tilted his head as he took in the unusual disarray of papers on Devlin's desk and frowned when he caught the name of the Okehampton solicitors at the top of one of the papers. "You in some kind of trouble?"

"Not me. Grace."

"You're running errands already, mummy's boy?"

Devlin knew Jamie had tagged the comment on the end to lighten the mood, but it still rankled. "Her dad made me executor of his will."

"And?"

Devlin ran a hand through his hair. "He put conditions on it."

Jamie's eyebrows raised. "Does Grace know?"

"I'm pretty certain she didn't when I mentioned it the other night. I'm meeting her at the solicitor's Monday."

His friend winced. "Don't envy you that job."

Devlin gave the solicitor's paperwork a sidelong look. "Neither do I."

Why did he ever agree with Geoff that if anything happened to him, he'd keep an eye out for Grace? *Because you didn't think it would be so soon.*

Jamie sat forward. "I often wondered why she never came back. Do you know?"

"No. All I know is that it was the one thing that really used to bother Geoff."

No matter what they talked about, Geoff would always bring the conversation back around to Grace. Where she was. What she was doing. A snippet from a magazine with one of her photos inside. It was strange to think that whenever Geoff had spoken about her, Devlin had pictured her as she was the last time he saw her, never really considering that she'd have grown up just as much as him.

Seeing her the other night had been a shock. Especially the attraction that hit him right in the solar plexus the moment his hands went around her arms in the darkness. In fighting against it, he'd reacted badly and had been on the wrong foot ever since.

"How come he chose you?"

Devlin gave him a wry smile. "Why? Are you jealous? Right now, I'd give the job up in a heartbeat if I had the choice."

Except, of course, they both knew that wasn't true. He might not be in a position to do anything about his attraction to Grace. But that didn't mean he couldn't hope their situation would change.

Not that it would go anywhere, even if things did change. As soon as he passed his fitness test, he'd be back out from behind this damned desk and back into the thick of it all. It was the only way to pay back for the people he'd let down before. Get it right next time, so no one else had to die.

Jamie cleared his throat. He was still waiting for Devlin to answer as to why Geoff had asked him in the first place.

Devlin blew out a sigh. "When I first came back from the hospital, aside from you and my mum and dad, he was my only regular visitor. I think he was lonely. Hell, maybe my mum put him up to it. I don't know. But he asked one day if I'd be the executor, and I said yes. He made it perfectly clear that if it wasn't me, then he'd ask someone else, and I didn't want to do that to Grace. If something happened to her dad, then I at least wanted her to have a friendly face."

Jamie smirked at the word friendly. It didn't matter how much Devlin denied his attraction, Jamie was never going to believe him. That was the problem with friends that knew you too well.

To his credit, Jamie tried to be more empathetic. "Except now with these conditions, you're the last person she wants to see."

"Exactly. That and I fucked up our first meeting."

Jamie's brow creased with an unspoken question, but Devlin was in no mood to expand further. He could tell himself it was to protect Grace's privacy, but his alter ego was quick to point out that it was guilt over making her cry. He hoped wherever Geoff was, he couldn't see.

"Can you say what the conditions are?"

Devlin pressed his lips together. "I'd rather Grace find out first."

Jamie moved towards the desk a little. "Come on. You know I can keep a secret."

Devlin shook his head and gave a bark of laughter. "Did anyone ever tell you that for an intelligence operative, you are the worst gossip in the world?"

Jamie's face broke into a broad smile. "Only about the delightful residents of Huntersford Leigh. Speaking of which, the pub quiz next week. Your folks and mine have already formed a team. I was going to ask Cal and Nathan to join ours."

Devlin lifted an eyebrow. "All male? Won't you get into trouble for being sexist or something?"

"Don't care. Jess will have Gabby, Tori, and probably even Grace on board, so I figure we'll be alright."

Devlin knew better than to argue. Jamie and Jess had been rivals since being captains of opposing rounders teams as kids. They still hadn't grown out of the bickering that ensued.

"Okay. I might be a little late. I want to get in some extra time at the gym. My CFT is in three weeks."

They might no longer work for the military directly, but passing Agema's combat fitness test was essential if he wanted to get back out in the field.

There was no need to explain further. Jamie understood that need better than anyone else he knew. He characterised the word workaholic. But then, his demons were a great deal darker than Devlin's.

Jamie rose from his chair and tapped the side of his head. "Duly noted," he said, before walking back out the door.

Grace leant against the granite rock, raised her head out of the shadows, and closed her eyes. Despite the low temperatures, the sun's rays warmed her face.

She needed this escape. As a child, coming to the tor had felt as if she were standing on top of the world. So high, no earthly problems could touch her.

Taking a deep breath, she relished the cold air hitting her lungs. The tension that had gripped her chest muscles into a tight spasm in the village store began to wane.

After the disaster in the store, she'd gone straight home and dug out her old walking boots from the back of the cupboard, grateful for the first time since she got back that her dad had never thrown anything out.

The climb up here had relieved some of her frustrations, and the breathtaking beauty of the moor had banished the encounter with the gossiping witches to a distant part of her mind.

The hard form of her camera beneath her fingers focused her chaotic thoughts. Photography had always cleared her head. It allowed her to shut out the noise and concentrate on capturing the perfect shot.

The only conflict she needed to face was through the lens finder. A temporary reprieve from a world that had always seemed at odds with her.

A cry in the wind overhead made her open her eyes. A kestrel hovered a little way from her, its pointed wings held out straight, barely fluttering as it poised above its prey. At this point on the tor, as the ground dropped away, it was almost as if she was up in the air with the majestic bird.

Raising her camera, she adjusted the lens and clicked. The kestrel swooped down, and she sat up, steadying her arm against her knee, and clicked again. Damn. She wished she'd thought to change the lens before coming up here, but she had so much pent up frustration to lose, she hadn't been thinking straight.

As the kestrel flew back up, she gave a silent hurrah for the creature that had escaped, leaving the bird to find another quarry. She tilted her lips in a half smile. Just like her today in the shop.

She lowered the camera and sighed. It was something she'd have to get used to. The chattering. The interference. It would only get worse once the truth was out. The police had confirmed her fears yesterday. Her father had been considerably over the legal alcohol limit when the accident occurred.

She should just be grateful that no one else had been injured or killed. But she couldn't shake the dread that gripped her every time she thought about it becoming public knowledge.

There would be no stopping the local paper from printing the cause of death. When that happened, the run-in today with Huntersford's very own coven would seem mild.

From the moment her mother became ill, stilted conversations, guarded looks, and sudden changes of subject had followed Grace wherever she went. It wasn't until she left for university that she managed to stop wanting to hide from everyone. Invisible in the anonymity of hundreds of other students who couldn't care less about her past, she finally relaxed.

But today proved that the notion of returning to Huntersford Leigh and remaining unscathed wasn't going to happen. She sighed and rubbed a hand over her face. If she had to put up with this much contempt just to buy a pint of milk, maybe she should have stayed away.

She leant back against the large boulder. Protected once more from the wind that whipped around her, she glanced across the moor. A glint far below in amongst the scrub and rocks caught her eye. Staring at the point where the hillside twisted a little, she was almost ready to put the shimmering down to her imagination when she saw it again. Leaning forward, she held up her camera to look through the viewfinder.

Fuck. Her nifty fifty wasn't much better than her own eyesight at this distance. If she hadn't been in such a temper, she would have picked up her camera bag and been able to switch the lens out for a zoom. The extra focal length would have given her a clearer view.

Lowering the camera, she squinted and tried to focus, but she couldn't distinguish anything in the moorland scrub. In her peripheral vision she saw another glint about twenty meters to the right. She turned and refocused her gaze, but still couldn't see any clearer.

A faint chill whispered across the back of her neck. Was someone watching her? She gave the possibility a half a second's serious thought before scoffing at herself. She was being ridiculous. It was more likely to be a piece of litter blowing in the breeze than someone crouched down in the bush scouring the tor with binoculars.

She stood up. It was time to make her way back down anyway. The sun was setting against a blanket of cloud rolling in across the sky. The horizon had taken on a dark lavender hue, and suddenly the moor no longer seemed to beckon her. Like a malevolent force, the encroaching dusky shadows urged her to leave. The wilderness she'd found so enchanting in the sunshine was no more.

She picked her way down off the tor and retraced the route she'd taken earlier. She slowed as she came to the spot where she'd seen the reflected light. There was nothing here now. She was about to continue down the path when she spotted something in a bramble. Squatting down to inspect it more closely, she found a navy piece of fabric that looked like it had been torn from some sort of waterproof material.

It wasn't proof that someone had been here earlier, but combined with the cold chill that skittered down her back, the find unnerved her. She straightened and continued back towards the village. Perhaps a warm supper would help her regain some of the confidence that had been shaken from her these last few days.

CHAPTER SIX

"What!" Grace bent forward in her chair, praying she hadn't heard the solicitor correctly.

"The will is quite clear, Miss Vaughan," said Mr Braithwaite. "The house cannot be sold for a year and you must remain in it. A maximum absenteeism of ninety days is allowed, with no single period of absenteeism to be more than two weeks."

"That's ridiculous." She turned to Devlin. His cool demeanour infuriated her even more. "And you knew about this?"

He gave a shrug of acknowledgement.

"And you didn't try to talk him out of it?"

He opened his mouth to speak, but she raised a hand to stop him. "Don't. Just don't say another word."

She was so angry she could barely think straight. To think she'd been worrying about her father ever since the police told her alcohol was the likely cause of the crash, and all the time he'd had this planned.

She'd been concerned about saving her father's reputation from being the target of village gossip and instead, now she would be the one. They were probably all laughing at her now.

She caught Devlin's impassive expression. No. That wasn't fair. She'd bet he hadn't told anyone that he was the executor, let alone the contents of the will. He'd seemed genuinely uncomfortable about it that first night. Even if he had been a jackass.

What was it he had said? Something about her being the one to put conditions on her relationship with her dad. The audacity of his words almost made her choke.

The solicitor shuffled the papers in front of him. "It really isn't as bad as it seems."

He was trying to pacify her, but all she wanted to do was rip the documents out of his hands and tear them into shreds.

She clenched her hands in her lap and forced herself to remain calm. "How so?"

"You can't sell the house until you have probate anyway and that can take several months. It's only a little longer until the year is out."

She narrowed her gaze. "And what about my work? What do I do in the meantime? It takes me two weeks sometimes just to reach my location."

"Take different assignments?"

Devlin's dry, sardonic tone did nothing to soothe her temperament. Any other time she might have conceded that it was a possibility, and certainly she could do a lot of the postproduction work from Huntersford Leigh. But this was an ambush, and she was in no mood to give anyone any leeway.

She levelled Devlin with a look that she hoped would silence him from offering further opinions, before refocusing on the solicitor.

"What happens if I don't? Does he get all the money?" She nodded her head towards Devlin. Why on earth had her father involved him in this anyway?

"No. It goes to a charity supporting the Dartmoor ponies."

"Great. Let them have it. They can sort out the house and every-thing. I don't need the money so badly I'm going to be held to this blackmail. What the hell was my father thinking?"

The solicitor sat back in his chair. "You're not being reasonable. It's obviously a shock. You should take some time to consider the will. It's quite a sum you're giving up."

Grace took a deep breath to cool her temper. This man was from a different era. Did he really think she was some overwrought, dis-traught daughter in need of financial advice?

With a cordiality she really didn't feel, she forced herself to respond calmly. "I can assure you things have never been clearer. Can I stay in the house while I finish the arrangements for my father's funeral?"

"Yes. Of course. It's yours unless you forfeit it under the terms of the will."

She turned to Devlin. "And what's your role in all this madness?"

The sardonic glint in his eyes should have been the warning that she wasn't going to like his response.

"I get to check up on you every day to see if you're there."

A gasp fell from her lips, and he gave her a tentative smile.

"Relax, Grace. I was joking. I report if the terms aren't being met. If you change your mind about staying, I promise I'll try to be reason-able, but your dad was pretty clear."

An icy chill swept through her. "Meaning?"

"If you're a day or so over the two weeks then fine, but if you go off for long durations, then I'll bring it to the attention of Mr Braithwaite."

Grace sat back in her chair and closed her eyes. A string of curses ran through her mind, half of them aimed at her father, the other half at Devlin. But it still left her with an overwhelming question. *Why?*

What was going through her father's mind when he made the will? Punishment for not coming back to see him? No. She didn't believe that. He understood, even if he wasn't happy with her decision.

"Miss Vaughan?" Her eyes flew open, meeting the solicitor's worried gaze. "You don't have to make a choice today. So long as you remain at the house, it stays yours."

The warning was clear. She really did want to tell them both to go to hell and move into a hotel in Exeter, but even in her distressed state she appreciated that to do so would be foolish. Besides, she needed time to go through the house and retrieve some of her mother's things. And maybe somewhere she'd find the answer to her father's ridiculous request.

Giving Devlin a sideways glance, she stood and picked up her handbag. She held out her hand to the solicitor. "Thank you, Mr Braithwaite. I'll let you know my decision in due course."

Devlin stood up next to her. He was so close she could feel the heat radiating from his body as the woody scent of his aftershave teased her nostrils. Her heart, already hammering in her chest from the stress of the meeting, sped up and her bag slipped through her fingers and fell to the floor with a thud.

She fumbled to pick it up, colliding with Devlin as he tried to help. Her humiliation complete, she let him help her upright again and prayed he didn't notice how much she was shaking.

As she reached out to take her bag from his hand, he pulled back, holding it slightly away. "If you want a lift back to Huntersford, I just need a few minutes alone with Mr Braithwaite."

So they could discuss monitoring her, no doubt. She would rather walk barefoot in freezing rain than get in a car with Devlin Judge right now.

"It's okay, thanks. I drove." Snatching her handbag from Devlin's grasp, she strode out of the solicitor's office with as much poise as she could muster.

Grace eyed the old writing desk with dread. On her way back from Okehampton, she'd decided she'd put off the task long enough.

There would be bills inside that needed paying, but until today, going through the contents had somehow felt like an invasion of Dad's privacy. Right now, she was too annoyed with him to care. Perfect timing.

Dragging out the chair from underneath the desk, she sat down and ran her hands over the worn wood. As her fingers hit the lock in the centre, she twisted the key and pulled the writing flap down.

The interior of the desk was just as she'd expected. Half a dozen cubbyholes stuffed full with pieces of paper and envelopes. A cheque book and a few sheets of writing paper were in the horizontal panel above and propped up at one end was a greeting card still wrapped in cellophane. The large text across the front was easy to read.

To a Darling Daughter on Her Birthday.

Tears welled in her eyes. No matter how hard they argued, he never missed her birthday. It wasn't for a couple of weeks, but he'd obviously gotten it early in time to reach her in Australia.

She reached for the card and picked it up. A teddy bear holding a bouquet of flowers stared back at her. She slumped back in the chair and tears flowed as memories of happier times flooded back.

When she was little, without fail they always used to go to the coast on her birthday. Walk along the beach at Dawlish Warren and into a little tea room afterwards to warm up. It was the one day a year she could eat whatever she liked. Ice cream for breakfast, fish fingers for lunch, and scones for tea. And as a special treat, her mum would make custard in a mug for her to take to bed and drink.

She closed her eyes and remembered the sound of the sea, the feel of the cold wind on her face and squealing with delight as her dad chased her across the sand.

The clock in the hallway chimed. She sat up and wiped her cheeks. She'd been wallowing there for nearly a half hour, staring into space. Moping about what might have been was never going to get things sorted.

Pulling out what looked to be the most recent set of bills, she went through them, putting to one side the ones already paid automatically by the bank, leaving her with just a couple that required immediate attention. She made a mental note to go into the bank at Exeter tomorrow to arrange for the account to be stopped.

Next, she picked up a pile of letters. Skimming through them, she recognised some of the names as distant relatives of her mother. Some had return addresses written on them, others didn't. She supposed she'd have to figure out a way to let them know about her dad's death, since he hadn't kept in touch with them after her mother died.

A photo fell out from the pile. Her mum stared back at her, smiling for the camera next to her dad. Behind them was an older couple she recognised from other photos she'd seen. She'd never known her grandparents. They'd died before she was born.

With her mum being an only child and her father having been brought up in care, it was going to be a lonely funeral. Grace let out a depressed sigh.

An envelope with a printed address caught her eye, and she snatched it up from the cubbyhole. The postmark was smudged, making the date unreadable. Opening the envelope, she pulled out a single sheet of paper, and an icy chill scuttled down her spine.

YOU KILLED HER.

The words were spaced in the centre of the page in block capitals. Somehow the small font size seemed to convey a more threatening tone than if it had been large with the words blazoned across the page.

She turned it over, even though the lightweight nature of the paper made it possible to see that the other side was blank. Placing it back on the writing table, she reached for the envelope. Her father had clearly ripped the top of the envelope with his usual disregard for the contents, which meant he hadn't expected to find anything so sinister inside.

She peered harder at the postmark, but the ink was impossible to read. It struck her then that there was no name on the envelope, just Moors Cottage, Huntersford Leigh. Her gaze drifted back to the piece of paper.

Who died? Had her father killed someone with his drinking? She dismissed the thought almost straight away. Her father would own up to something so monumental.

Did it have anything to do with his death? Was it suicide? Her stomach churned with the thought. She leant her elbows on the desk and placed her head in her hands. "Dad, what have you done?"

Her mind raced, searching for anything that would explain the note, but came up empty. Should she show it to the police, or was it better just to avoid any more fodder for the rumour mill and let it go? Maybe it was nothing.

But then why had her dad kept it? It would have been easy enough to throw it on the woodburner and have the note literally disappear into smoke.

She stared down at the piece of paper, trying to comprehend what it meant. A rapping on the living room door startled her. She looked up and met Devlin's curious gaze. Great, just what she needed.

"Sorry. I didn't mean to spook you. I knocked on the front door, but you didn't hear."

"Maybe I was ignoring you." She stood. The last thing she needed was Devlin making himself at home on the sofa.

He glanced down at her hand. "What's that?"

It was only at his sharp tone that she realised she was still holding the letter.

CHAPTER SEVEN

Grace snatched her hand behind her. "Nothing."

Devlin gritted his teeth. He hadn't seen it clearly before she moved it out of his vision, but one line in the middle of a single piece of paper was never good news. "Grace, show me the note."

"No. You're not in charge of my life, Devlin, just Dad's will."

She turned and placed it face down on the writing table behind her. Unless he was going to storm past, it was out of his reach. He debated for a split second, but common sense won. He was already on her shit list. No need to make it worse. He'd get to see the note, eventually.

He exhaled. "Fine. If you change your mind, let me know."

"I won't."

She stared back at him defiantly. He didn't doubt her intent, but he'd find another way. Perhaps distraction would work?

He held out the envelope he'd been clutching. "I, on the other hand, am happy to share. The solicitor forgot to give you a copy of the papers."

"Thanks." She reached out and took it from him, eyeing the contents warily.

"He said he'd write to you formally, just to clarify everything that was said at the meeting."

Two bright spots of colour appeared in her pale cheeks. He could understand her anger. Coming home only to have the rug ripped out from under you must be hard.

She'd obviously been crying before he barged in, and he wanted to reach out and give her a hug. But that was a gesture from their friendship of old, now consigned most definitely to the past.

They didn't even have the uneasy truce he thought they'd had after bumping into each other in the car park. Especially after the meeting at the solicitors, where she'd riled him so much he hadn't been able to resist taking a cheap shot at her.

It wasn't like him to be so petty, but the Grace Vaughan of today had him so off kilter, he didn't recognise himself.

Not for the first time that day, he cursed Geoff and his will. He cleared his throat. "It will get easier."

She eyed him sharply. "What will?"

"Coming home."

A frown marred her brow, and she looked down. "What would you know about it? You're a war hero. I'm the girl people whisper about."

The heavy weight in his chest made it hard to speak. "I'm not."

"Not what?"

He exhaled. "A hero."

"Yeah, sure. Dad told me all about your bravery medal."

"It doesn't feel like it when one of your team dies because you made an error." He hadn't meant to say it, but she pushed him too far sometimes.

She stuttered for a moment, clearly trying to grasp everything he'd not said. She lifted her chin and met his gaze, and his heart caught for a beat. The glistening in her eyes said it all. She understood. The pain. The loss. The guilt.

Her expression softened. "Sorry. I didn't realise."

"It's okay. I don't talk about it." He lifted his hand, gesturing towards the village. "And everyone here only sees what they want to."

A faint smile crossed her lips. "And makes up what they don't know." She held up the envelope he'd given her. "Still, this will certainly give everyone something to talk about. Too bad I won't be around to hear it."

He scrubbed a hand over his face. "Don't leave because of the will."

"Really? You sure about that? Because I could have sworn you were leading the charge to hasten my departure."

She turned away from him and placed the envelope on top of the note, firmly pushing the two out of his reach. "Although the Weird Sisters are doing a good job of beating you to first place."

The side of his mouth slid up at her mention of their childhood nickname for the village gossips. If he remembered correctly, it was Jess that had started calling them that after she first read Macbeth. The name had stuck in their little group.

"What did they do now?"

Grace rolled her eyes. "Well, they agree with you that I'm a bad daughter. But that's because I'm having Dad cremated, not buried."

"Ignore them."

"So you're not going to deny that you think I'm a bad daughter?"

Fuck. He'd walked into that one. "I told you before, I never thought that of you."

She looked skywards as if she was praying for patience. "I tried to take no notice, but it's a little hard when they've got you cornered in the store."

Devlin sighed. They could be vicious when they wanted to be. "You should talk to my mum. Ask her for some tips. When I first came home, she used to storm into my house muttering curses I didn't think she knew after listening to all their helpful advice about how to take care of her mentally unstable son.”

Grace gasped. “Were you?”

“Unstable? No.” Guilt-ridden and desperate to get back out there and kill the bastards that blew up his friend. Maybe. “But it didn’t stop their cruel words from getting to her.”

“Your poor mum.” Concern was written all her over face, and for a moment Devlin saw the Grace of old. The one who wore her heart on her sleeve and cared deeply about even the smallest creature.

“She soon put them straight, and they left her alone.” He lifted his chin in the direction of the documents behind her. “Are you going to show me the note?”

“What note?”

“Grace.” Even though he knew his warning tone would rile her further, he couldn’t hide his frustration.

She glared back at him. “It’s nothing Dev. I was going through the writing desk and came across it. It’s probably just a bit of nonsense sent by some nosy parker in the village stirring up trouble. Forget all about it.”

“A threatening note is not nothing.”

Tilting her head, she dismissed his concerns with a wave of her hand. “It’s not threatening. It’s a statement.”

He crossed his arms. “That’s semantics, and you know it.”

Her hand went to her neck. She ran her fingers over the chain she’d worn there since her mother died. “It doesn’t matter now anyway, does it? He’s dead. It’s irrelevant.”

Her denial was at odds with her actions. It was clear she was wondering what the hell it was about, but she was never going to admit it. And he couldn’t blame her.

Dark shadows were forming under her eyes. Now wasn't the time to push the point. She'd said it herself. Any threat was moot if Geoff wasn't around. But that still didn't mean it was nothing.

He turned just as he got to the hallway. "Okay. Have it your way, Grace. You know where I am if you change your mind."

Not that he expected her to. Fortunately, he was fairly certain he'd be able to persuade his mum to do a little snooping for him.

Once Devlin had left, Grace sat back in the chair, folded everything into the writing desk except for the outstanding bills and locked the flap shut.

Removing the key, she placed it on a shelf in between a couple of her mother's gardening books. It had been over a week since her father's death. The letter had been there all this time without causing a commotion. What harm could waiting do?

She didn't want to stir up a hornet's nest unnecessarily. There would be enough gossip, between the cause of the accident and the conditions of her inheritance, without pouring more fuel on the fire.

But somewhere between cursing Devlin and swearing at her father for making the will in the first place, a niggle of doubt had crept into her mind.

And now it was there, it refused to budge.

The police had said her father was significantly over the legal limit for driving and that it would have been a contributing factor to the accident. At the time, she hadn't wanted to seem disloyal to him, so she'd said nothing. But that was her concern. That amount of alcohol was nothing for her father. So why had he crashed?

He could have easily swerved around a stray pony on the road. But they tended to stay away from the tarmac in the first place. She frowned. Had the alcohol started to affect him more? Was he sick? He'd seemed okay when she video called him last month before she started her current project. But had something changed?

A knock at the front door startled her. She looked up at the mantlepiece clock. It was nearly six. She made her way to the door just as someone knocked again.

"I'm coming!" She threw open the door, dreading that Devlin had returned for some reason.

Instead, a dark-haired beauty stood before her. The tresses Grace had always been jealous of were tied back in a ponytail that barely contained the bouncing curls. It seemed like an eternity since they had sat in class together.

"Jess!" As her face cracked into a wide grin, Grace realised it was the first time in days that a genuine smile had crossed her lips.

"Hi. Sorry if I'm interrupting."

"No, not at all." She held the door open. "Do you want to come in? The living room's a mess, but we can sit in the kitchen."

Her friend's brown eyes lit up with mirth. "And talk about boys! Just like old times."

Laughter bubbled up inside of Grace. She'd forgotten how Jess' vivacious personality infused everything. If only everyone was as happy to see her again. "I've had enough of men for the moment. How about you tell me more about this jewellery business Dad told me all about?"

The smile on Jess' face froze, and suddenly Grace was engulfed in her friend's embrace. "Oh, Gracie. I'm so sorry. In the excitement of seeing you, I forgot why you're here."

Grace hugged her back, her chest tightened as she held her tears in check. "It's okay. I'd rather smiles and happy memories than dwell on the what-might-have-beens."

Her friend leant back and studied her seriously for a moment. "Still looking forward constantly? I've warned you about that. Sometimes it's good to stand still for a moment." She hooked Grace's arm in hers and pulled her into the house. "Come on. You can start by telling me all about the bronzed hunks you left behind in Australia."

As Grace made tea, Jess peppered her with questions over the places she'd visited for work.

"Don't you get tired of all that travelling?"

"Not really. I'm too busy to notice."

Placing two mugs of tea on the table, she took the chair opposite Jess. "What about you? Dad said you have your own shop now."

"It's really just the old butcher's shop converted into a work studio, with a few glass cabinets I managed to pick up from an auction in Okehampton. But it's great in the summer for catching the tourist trade, and beats having to do several markets a week. Actually, I was going to ask you to give me some tips on taking better photos of the pieces I want to sell online."

"Of course I will. Is that one of your pieces you're wearing now? It's beautiful."

Jess straightened in her chair and held it out for Grace to examine it closer. "Yes. Always my own. I figure I'm the best advocate of my jewellery. Although I'm sure people around here get sick of me talking about it." She gave Grace a sheepish smile and took a sip of her tea. "Your dad was always really sweet though."

Grace sighed. At some point, she was going to have to come clean about his drinking. If she'd known coming home was going to be so complicated, maybe she would have stayed in Australia. Immediately she nixed the thought. They might have had their differences, but she couldn't imagine not coming back to Huntersford Leigh one last time to say goodbye.

She glanced up. Jess was looking expectantly at her, and she realised she hadn't responded to the comment about her dad.

"Sorry. It's been a lot to take in."

She sensed that Jess wanted to say more, but thankfully unlike Dev, her friend changed the subject instead.

"Oh, my god. I almost forgot the real reason I came."

Grace eyed her warily. She didn't think she could take any more surprises.

"We need you on our team for the pub quiz on Thursday."

Her stomach clenched and she turned away to hide her face. "No. It's too much, too soon. I'm not sure I can face everyone in one go."

Jess reached across the table and squeezed Grace's forearm. "Pleeease. Look at it this way—you can say hi to everyone without having to have the same long, boring conversation about what you've been up to."

Grace looked up at the ceiling. She knew what Jess meant, even if it sounded like a backhanded compliment. Levelling a glare at Jess, she cocked her head. "So you're doing me a favour by inviting me to bolster your quiz team?"

Jess raised her brows hopefully. "Did it work?"

She groaned. Jess was right—she'd have nonstop visitors dropping by to see her otherwise. At least this way she got it all done in one night. "Okay. Maybe you do have a point."

"Yay! We are so gonna beat the boys."

Grace chuckled. "I've been gone twelve years and nothing's changed. Except that at least a quiz is less energetic than a game of rounders."

"Oh, plenty's changed. Just you wait and see." She picked up her phone and slipped it into her back pocket as she stood-up, then pulled on her coat. "It starts at eight. We meet at a quarter to for drinks and to grab a table. Text me when you leave here and I'll make sure I'm there to defend you from the maundering hordes."

"Thanks, Jess." She rose from her chair and gave her friend a wry smile. "I think."

"Thanks for the tea. See you hun." Jess bent over and kissed her on the cheek, giving her a half hug at the same time. "It's so good to have you back."

Grace only wished she could say the same thing.

Chapter Eight

The loud rapping of the door knocker no longer took Grace by surprise. This was the third time she'd heard it in as many hours. Maybe Jess was right, that going to the pub quiz would get everybody's curiosity out of the way.

Although by tomorrow night she didn't imagine there would be many people left in the village that she hadn't seen. There were so many people knocking at the front door and declaring that they were just dropping by, the house was starting to feel like Piccadilly Circus.

It might not have been quite so bad if the house hadn't been in such disarray. Yesterday, she'd taken the kitchen apart, washing down every nook and cranny until there wasn't a speck of dirt to be found. She'd worked through until nearly one in the morning trying to exhaust herself into sleep.

This afternoon she was tidying the living room of the clutter that had built up over the years. At some point she'd have to tackle her dad's bedroom, but for the moment she couldn't even bring herself to step inside.

She checked out her reflection in the hall mirror before reaching for the door lock. Whoever it was would just have to accept her dishevelled state. How else was she going to get the house clean, if she had to look smart for every visitor?

She threw open the door, and her heart sank at the sight of the man on her doorstep. "Devlin, how delightful." She tilted her head, taking in his casual attire. "And to what do I owe this visit? A spot inspection?"

His jaw tightened a little. She'd annoyed him. Good. He deserved it.

"I came to check you were all right."

She was tempted to tell him to go to hell, but instead she just raised a hand and let it fall to her side. "As you can see, I'm just peachy."

"I wondered if I could come in for a minute?"

She moved to one side, and he stepped into the hallway. He looked into the living room and frowned. "You're packing?"

The accusation in his tone raised her hackles even more.

"No, I'm tidying up and putting away some things, which should have been done years ago. At least that way it will make it easier to keep clean. You can inspect the boxes if you're worried about me taking something I shouldn't."

A hissing sound emitted from between his lips. "Grace, you know I didn't mean it that way."

"Do I? You were pretty clear in the solicitor's office." He'd even gloated, if she recalled correctly.

"I was being a jerk. I'm sorry. I'm not going to lie, I will take my responsibility as executor seriously, but I won't stop you from taking things from the house. The will says the house goes to charity, not the contents."

So he'd gone through the will enough to work out the small print? She'd couldn't help but wind him up further, which probably made her as much of a bitch as he was being a dick. But she was beyond caring. "That's very magnanimous of you."

His wince at her sarcastic tone made the churlish little girl inside of her feel better.

He strode across the living room to stare out of the window at the back garden for a few moments before turning around and leaning against the windowsill. "I give up. I can't win. I have no idea why your dad made his will as it is, but you can't fault me for carrying out his wishes."

Petulance forgotten, her blood pressure peaked. "Actually, I can. Didn't you think to question him when he told you about it?"

He straightened bolt upright as if she'd hit him. "Of course I did. Do you know what he said? That he'd find someone else if I didn't want to do it." He stretched out a hand towards her. "I couldn't do that to you, Grace. At least if I was in charge, then I could ensure it was fair."

"There's nothing fair about that will. How do you think I feel, having to ask if I can have something that was my mother's? Something that my father would have given freely when he'd been alive."

Devlin cocked his head and quirked an eyebrow. "If only you were ever here to ask for it."

A coldness swept over her. It was just as well she wasn't still holding the vase she'd been wrapping before he arrived, otherwise she'd have thrown it at him. Who the hell did Devlin Judge think he was?

He walked over to where she stood and placed his hands on her shoulders. "Sorry." His voice softened. "That was unforgivable."

He met her gaze with an intensity that had always unnerved her when they were younger. But his apology was too late. The guilt from the truth in his words stuck in her throat. She raised her arms to force his hands away and walked over to the fireplace, taking a deep, calming breath.

The warmth of the fire did little to ward off the chill that had settled over her. To think she'd almost relented and shown him the note. Once upon a time she would have sought his advice, but not now. Everything was so fucked up. How had she possibly thought that she'd be able to breeze in and out of Huntersford Leigh unscathed?

For years she'd blamed her father's drinking for not coming home, but had she been deluding herself all this time? Was the real reason that she was too afraid of facing her own demons. Of what people might say or think?

Her mobile started ringing loudly on the mantelpiece. She pounced on the distraction and glanced up at Devlin. "Sorry. I need to take this."

She swiped to answer the call. "David! It's so great to hear from you."

Devlin stalked towards the door that Grace had pulled close behind her as she stepped out of the room. He didn't care if it was rude to eavesdrop. The way her face lit up as she answered the call was a punch in the gut.

Who the hell was David?

Her dad had never mentioned a boyfriend.

It was the first time he'd seen her genuinely smile since she returned. It transformed her face. She looked radiant, beautiful, and it dawned on him that he hadn't seen her this happy in years. He shifted uneasily at the depressing thought.

Through the slit in the door, he could see her leaning against the kitchen counter, taking down notes on what looked like the back of an envelope.

"That sounds amazing. When were you thinking about scheduling it?" She held the phone away from her ear and tapped at the screen.

"Mid-February, if you can swing it?" a deep voice with a South London accent answered, while she scrolled through what Devlin presumed was her calendar.

"Perfect. I've an opening from the fifteenth." She tapped the screen and held the phone back to her ear. "How long do you anticipate the shoot to take?"

She held a pencil to her mouth as she listened to the response. The gesture drew Devlin's attention to her full bottom lip and for a fraction of a second he wondered what it would be like to capture it with his own. He shut the thought down as fast as it had come from nowhere.

She moved the pencil back to the paper and jotted down some more notes. "Great. I can't wait." She switched the phone to balance it between her ear and shoulder and reached up to get a glass from the cupboard above.

The movement made her sweater rise up, revealing a tantalising glimpse of her stomach, and Devlin stifled a groan. He was supposed to be eavesdropping, but he was rapidly turning into a peeping tom.

"Are you sure it's not too inconvenient? It would make it so much easier to stay with you."

Devlin scrutinised at her face. Still smiling. Still looking like someone who had been given something they'd always wanted. Shit.

"That's just so generous of you, David. I can't wait. It will be like old times."

No. Fucking. Way.

His chest tightened at her gushing tone. He remembered clearly how she used to chatter animatedly about the wildlife on the moor when they were young. How come she never talked to him like that anymore?

He scrubbed a palm over his face. *Oh, yeah. Thanks Geoff.*

She started to wrap up the call, and he moved away from the door.

The smile on her face vanished as she came into the room and saw him standing by the window again.

"Job prospect?" There was no point in pretending he hadn't over-heard.

"Yes, for an old friend."

"Not too far away, I hope."

The flash of annoyance in her eyes told him what an arse he was being, but he just didn't seem to be able to help himself when he was around her.

"Not that it's any of your business, but it's for a zoo near London. I'm sure I can catch a train back to suit your uptight schedule."

He took a step forward. "But that's where you're wrong. It is most definitely my business."

She took a step towards him too, her back ramrod straight, eyes blazing. "Oh no, don't think you can be in charge of my life, Devlin Judge. I stand by what I said at the solicitors. You can all go to hell. The house and whatever money Dad's got in his account will all go to the damn charity before I bow to your wishes. I'll even throw in a free photo shoot of the ponies just to show them there's no hard feeling."

He wanted to shake her for being so stubborn. Instead, he ran a hand through his hair and gripped the back of his neck. "Do you think your dad wanted you to throw everything away?"

She raised her hands and then let them fall to her sides. "I don't know. You had all the long conversations with him, you tell me."

She'd thrown his words back at him, and he deserved it. He was just as clueless as she was as to why Geoff had changed his will.

Before he could say another word, she turned on her heel and marched over to where she'd been sorting through various objects when he arrived.

She sat in amongst the things and resumed her task, not looking up as she said, "Don't let the door hit you on your way out."

He'd come here to apologise, but all he'd done was confirm that he was still a jackass. How was it possible that he could talk people into giving away information every day, but fuck it up so easily when it came to conversing with Grace?

Chapter Nine

Grace took a sip of her wine. Wedged up against the window at the end of the table, she was grateful that Jess had made sure she was partially hidden from the majority of people.

The Arms was packed tonight. From what she'd gathered, this was unusual for a cold January night. The quiz had brought out all the locals. Unfortunately, one of them was Devlin.

She knew she should have expected him to be there, but her breath had caught when she looked across the room and saw him. She was still annoyed about the meeting at the solicitors. If he thought he could lord it over her everywhere she went, he'd have another think coming.

The will had her in an absolute quandary. She'd spent the last few days seesawing from telling Dev and the solicitor to shove it, to being more reasonable and just braving it out. After all, she didn't have to stay in Huntersford Leigh after the year was up.

The woman at the end of their table, who Jess had introduced as Suzanne, broke into a smile as someone approached their table. "Gabby! I thought you weren't going to make it."

Grace craned her neck to get a better look. Gabby still had that sweet, innocent expression she'd had as a child. Her long blonde hair only emphasised the angelic look. Not that it fooled anyone that knew her.

"Sorry I'm late. I had an emergency the other side of Postbridge."

"Well, at least you made it. Come on, budge up Jess, and make room." Suzanne created space for Gabby to sit down. "We could have done with your animal knowledge ten minutes ago. Fortunately, our resident Oz expert was able to come to our rescue."

Suzanne nodded towards where Grace sat and Gabby's eyes widened as she caught sight of her. "Oh my god! It's true, you're back." She jumped up and reached across the table to hug Grace, squeezing her so hard it took her by surprise.

"Careful, Pint-Size," Jess said, lifting an arm to separate them. "I promised Grace I wouldn't let anyone maul her."

Gabby rolled her eyes at the childhood nickname. "I'm not just anyone."

"No. But you weren't the girl she sat next to in class."

"That's because you all went off to secondary school and left me with Mrs Hargreaves in a class of one. I still haven't forgiven you." Gabby plumped down on her seat as if she was deeply affronted.

Grace smiled as their banter brought back old memories. Huntersford's primary school had been a small room at the side of the village hall with a single teacher, Mrs Hargreaves. The older children sat at the back and the younger ones at the front. The number of pupils never grew beyond nine in total the entire time she was there.

Except for that year Mrs Smith's nephew came down from up north and stayed with her for a few months while her sister had treatment for cancer. Gosh. She hadn't thought about him in an age.

Jess gave Gabby's ponytail a friendly tug. "At least you were brainy and got moved up a year early. Hasn't done you any harm."

"Hey, that's cheating. Only four people a team," came a call from across the room.

Jess looked over her shoulder and rolled her eyes. "Yeah, Jamie? Afraid you'll lose?"

Tori started to stand. "I'm sorry guys, I can bow out if you want. I didn't realise when I asked if I could join, that you were already up to numbers."

Jess waved her back down. "Oh, ignore them. It's for charity for Christ's sake. Sometimes I think they forget that the rest of us have our own minds and lives that don't need their interference."

"Attitude is a prerequisite for one of those jobs," said Gabby.

Grace frowned. "What do you mean?"

"The one where they come out of the military, start working for a defence contractor in Exeter and are really vague about what they do," Jess explained.

Gabby leant forward across the table to Grace and spoke in a low voice. "What does Dev say he does?"

The others moved closer to hear her answer.

"I haven't asked him." No. She had been too tied up in her worries to ask him how he felt about leaving the army. Years ago, it would have been precisely the kind of thing they might have discussed.

Jess placed her elbows on the table. "What the hell have you been talking about?"

Grace winced a little. "It's complicated."

Four pairs of eyes stared at her, but she just shrugged. She didn't know where to begin, even if she had been inclined to tell. Although judging by the daggers Jess was giving her, she wouldn't be able to keep quiet for long.

Eventually she broke eye contact and glanced over to the table where Jamie and Devlin sat across the room. "Still think they're in charge around here, though."

"Yeah, well, we let them have their illusions," chimed in Suzanne, holding up her glass, and they all clinked it with their own in agreement.

"Do we know if we're ahead?" Grace asked, eager to move the conversation away from her.

"No, because Pete's a mean son of a bastard who won't let anyone know until the end. Not even a hint," Jess complained.

Grace wished she had some of Jess' bravado. Her friend didn't even show a hint of chagrin as Pete reached in to collect their empty glasses off the table.

"I keep telling you, love, not knowing makes it more exciting. If you knew they were ten points ahead now, you'd give up, wouldn't you?"

Jess' jaw dropped and her eyes widened. "Are they?"

He reached for the last glass. "Sorry, can't say." He chuckled in delight at Jess' groan of dismay before walking back to the bar.

Gabby grinned. "Pub quiz always brings out your competitive streak."

"What, are we all eight again suddenly?" Jess bristled.

The five of them fell silent for a moment, before Tori's quietly spoken "yes" had them falling about in hoots of laughter.

Devlin met Grace's gaze across the pub and mouthed "hi" to her. She turned her head away as if she hadn't seen him. He needed to figure this out. He didn't usually make such tactical errors as he'd done with her.

But she sent his blood pressure spiking every time they talked. He wasn't sure if it was the frustration of pressuring her to stay and comply with a dead man's wish when she clearly wanted to leave. Or fighting his own instinct, which was to thrust his fingers in her hair and kiss her senseless even though he had every intention of leaving himself.

He was fairly certain that Geoff didn't mean for him to do either of those things when he'd asked him to look after Grace.

Callum's raised voice drew his attention back to the quiz. "I get at least one of the questions on *Only Connect* right every week. Shut up and write the answer down. I'm telling you, it's correct." He stabbed at the paper on the table in front of them. His brother Nate gave up the fight and wrote it down.

It was the final question of the night and Devlin couldn't say that he wasn't glad.

Grace stood and headed towards the bar. Maybe now was a good opportunity to take advantage of neutral territory and have a normal conversation for once.

He stood up and gathered the empty pint glasses on the table. "Same again?"

Jamie craned his neck to check out the rest of the pub and smothered a laugh. "Wondered what it might take to get your to open your wallet, mate."

Devlin silently cursed Jamie. He'd already given a knowing look when Devlin made him switch places earlier so he could face the bar. Fortunately, Callum and Nate were still too busy arguing about the final answer to notice.

As he approached the bar, a man and a woman came in through the salon door that led to the other side of the pub the locals rarely used. Tourists, judging by their attire. Their expressions alight with excitement and he guessed their flush faces had more to do with exertion than the warmth of the pub.

Still pouring a pint for Harry Jones, Pete turned his head towards them. "What can I do you for?"

"We're not sure." The couple glanced at each other nervously. Then the woman spoke. "We were heading along the lane, when a woman ran out in front of us."

"It was so last minute we thought we might have hit her, so we stopped and got out of the car and searched and searched, but couldn't see anything. No trace of her at all," said the man.

"Just by the Please Drive Carefully sign?" Harry asked, his expression deadpan.

"Yes. What should we do?"

"Nothing," said Pete. "That'll be Idonea. Well known she is around these parts."

Never one to miss out on embellishing Pete's claims, Harry continued to chime in. "The pub's named after her. The Idonea Arms. Fiercer than Boadicea, they say."

Pete straightened up and handed Harry his pint. "You staying locally?" he asked them.

"Yes. Just up the road at the B&B," said the woman as she started to unzip her jacket.

Pete picked up two glasses, reached over to the line of bottles behind him and poured a couple of scotches from the optics. "Here, have a drink on the house. You look like you need it. You can leave your car here tonight and walk back in the morning. It will be safe enough."

Devlin tuned out their response and turned towards Grace at the bar. Her eyes sparkled with mirth at Pete and Harry's double act, and her mouth twitched as she suppressed a smile.

"Hi."

"Hi, Dev."

The smile was gone. His name was a sigh on her lips and not in a good way.

"How did you get on with the quiz?"

She shrugged and turned to get Pete's attention, waving a twenty-pound note in her hand.

Never one to surrender, he tried again. "That last question was hard. Nathan and Callum are still arguing over the answer."

She peeked over his shoulder to where they sat, and a glimmer of amusement returned to her eyes. "Those brothers have been fighting since before they could talk."

Devlin chuckled. "When I first came back six months ago, I couldn't believe how much had changed. Shops gone. New houses built. The White Hart closed. Then I bumped into those two walking down here for a pint, and I realised that I was just looking at the surface. The things I loved about Huntersford were still there."

Grace arched an eyebrow. "Trying to sell it to me now?"

"Is it working?"

She leant in and he was powerless to resist breathing in the heady scent of her that had clouded his judgement ever since that first night she came home.

"If you think two boneheaded brothers are going to change my mind, you're as deluded as them."

The insult probably should have been like a bucket of cold water. But this close to her, all he wanted to do was kiss the side of her upturned lips.

His wavering self-control was saved as she moved away and placed her order with Pete.

"You do him a disservice, you know."

Her brow marred with a frown as she watched Pete pour the wine. "Who?"

"Callum. He turned out to be one hell of a good doctor."

She leaned in again and spoke in a low tone that he might have found sexy if it wasn't being used to berate him. Ah hell, it was sexy, and he didn't care.

"I'm sure Callum is excellent, but as we both know, I'm not going to be here long enough to need his services."

"You could give us all a chance." A couple of days ago, he'd have been baiting her, but now something inside of him wanted her to stay. But the sardonic glint in her eyes told him there was little chance of that happening.

"You're forgetting I've already been reacquainted with the Weird Sisters. This is my life, Devlin, and how I choose to lead it is up to me. Not you. Not my dad. Me."

Before he could respond, she handed her money to Pete, picked up the glasses of wine in front of her, and headed back to her table.

A few minutes later he returned to his own table, four pints in hand.

"And? Can you tell me about the will yet?" Jamie asked in a hushed undertone.

Devlin lifted his pint, taking a sip before coming to a decision. "Remember, you cannot tell anyone unless Grace decides to say something."

Jamie levelled him with a look. This was nothing compared to the information they handled every day. And, despite what Grace probably thought, he didn't want to do anything that would cause her pain. But at the same time, he valued Jamie's opinion on the matter. He had a feeling that, mixed up in his attraction to Grace, he'd missed a critical point.

He placed his pint back on the table. "She doesn't get to keep the house unless she stays here for a year."

"Seriously?" A faint trace of shock tainted Jamie's response.

"Yep."

"And you're the executor."

Now he sounded slightly amused, and it pissed Devlin off.

"Mm-hmm."

"Geoff must have really hated you." Jamie's broad grin took the heat out of his words.

"Why do you say that?"

"He basically said *Hey, Dev, would you look after my daughter, but in a really shitty way?*" Jamie shook his head in disbelief. "And she's still talking to you?"

"Barely."

"No wonder she never came back."

"What do you mean?"

"Imagine if anything happened to your old man, and he left you the farm on the condition you continue on with it."

Devlin looked over to where his dad and mum sat, the pair of them deep in conversation with Callum and Nate's parents. "He'd never do it. He knows farming doesn't interest me."

"Exactly. He listens. Lets you make your own decisions. What you're saying sounds like bullshit. Like Geoff is trying to control her from beyond the grave."

"I don't think he meant it like that. I think he felt he pushed Grace away, and he wanted her to have a home again."

"By holding her hostage?"

Fuck. Put like that, no wonder Grace didn't want to talk to him. Was that how she felt? He took a deep breath. "There's something else."

But he didn't get to tell Jamie about the note. Callum interrupted them just as Pete announced the winners.

Chapter Ten

Grace lay in bed listening to the wind as it howled around the cottage. Every time she closed her eyes she replayed her conversation with Devlin in the pub. She'd never considered that coming back to Huntersford had been hard for him. Her dad had said he'd been injured, but there was no evidence of it now when she looked at him.

He'd filled out in the years since she last saw him. Broad shoulders, muscles her hands itched to touch even when he was being annoying. The teenage Devlin she remembered, she'd thought of as a friend. But the man he was now had her confused. Was her going toe to toe with him over her dad's will more about resisting her attraction to him? Not to mention avoiding dissecting the guilt that was plaguing her over her father's death.

She'd relaxed tonight for the first time in days. Ironically, probably assisted by a couple of glasses of wine. But she couldn't shake the feeling that maybe she and her dad should have put their differences behind them. Coming back had dredged up so many memories. She hadn't just lost her dad, but her mother too, all over again.

As a teenager she'd dreaded people finding out about her father, convinced she'd lose friends. But would Jess and Gabby really be so shallow as to blame her for her father's failings?

They probably wouldn't have been back then, and that certainly wasn't her impression of the two people she'd reconnected with tonight. She was basing all of her fear on her teenage self.

The truth was all going to come out soon anyway. If she faced up to it now maybe she'd at least stay in touch with her friends when she left Huntersford this time.

She raised herself up and punched her pillow a couple of times. She'd probably sleep better too if she stopped worrying. She closed her eyes again and immediately Devlin's image appeared. Groaning, she turned onto her side and curled up. She needed to find a way to banish him from her dreams too.

Outside the wind was gaining traction. It had whipped around her on the walk back from the pub and she'd warmed herself with thoughts of hot summer days spent lounging around by the river and playing pooh sticks with Jess on the bridge.

A faint smile crept across her lips, and she closed her eyes again.

Was that a noise outside? She held her breath, trying to be as silent as possible to distinguish the sound more clearly from the trees rustling in the wind.

If she were a paranoid person, she'd swear someone was moving around outside.

Annoyed with herself for giving into her fears, she rolled over. For Christ's sake, she'd slept in the jungle with a lot less than the bricks and mortar that protected her now. It was just that note that had given her the jitters.

But at least in the jungle she'd had a guard with her to scare away the animals and poachers. Here her nearest neighbours were Anna and Mick, half a mile up the lane.

Sighing, reached out and grabbed her phone. Ten minutes to midnight. Too late to be someone making their way back from the pub.

Had someone heard about her father's death and thought the cottage might be empty?

Swinging her legs over the side of the bed, she stood and crept over to the window. Slowly she lifted the curtain to one side. The clouds were thicker now, but every so often a break gave her a glimpse of the garden bathed in moonlight. She peered through the glass but couldn't discern anything out of the ordinary.

A loud bang startled her. She dropped the curtain and jumped back, her hand on her chest, her heart pounding in her throat. *What the fuck?* The noise came again and she opened the curtain a little. The shed door swung in the wind, banging back onto its wooden frame.

She let out a shaky laugh. She *was* being paranoid. Slipping into her old dressing gown that she'd found earlier in her wardrobe, she walked downstairs and grabbed the torch from the shelf as she passed before opening the back door.

Jesus, the wind was biting. Pulling the dressing gown tighter and wishing she'd put on a coat, she hurried over to the shed and forced the door shut. Her cold fingers battled with the lock as the door moved forcibly in the gusting wind. Tomorrow she'd get a padlock to make sure it couldn't fly open again.

Once the lock was secure, she scanned the garden for other hazards. With nothing else obviously about to take flight in the wind, she started to head back inside, but a movement near the side of the house sent a chill down her spine.

She lifted the torch and shone it in that direction, but all she saw was her hire car.

"Who's there?" Fear tightened her throat and her voice came out as barely more than a whisper. She coughed and shouted out again. "Is somebody there?"

Only the wind answered her.

Hoping if someone had been there she'd scared them off, she stepped towards the car. Her breath caught as she saw two deep scratches down one side. In the dirty glass on the driver's window, someone had written Stay Away From H.

She'd obviously interrupted whoever it was, but that didn't stop the shock from taking hold. Running back to the house, she locked the door and removed the key, placing it on the other side of the kitchen. If someone broke the glass in the upper panel of the door, she didn't want the key to be within easy reach.

Still holding the torch, she systematically searched every room to ensure she was the only one in the house before wedging a kitchen chair under the handle of the back door. The front door had two solid bolts that would slow down any intruder.

Stoking the fire into life, she poured a large brandy from a bottle she found at the back of her dad's drinks cabinet and sat down in front of the flames. As the amber liquid burned its way down her throat, fear turned to anger. Stay away from here? She didn't even want to be in Huntersford Leigh in the first place.

She grabbed the comforter from the other chair and snuggled down, keenly listening for any sound inside and outside the cottage. Sleep wasn't going to come now, but at least in front of the fire she'd be warm.

Grace turned the lens to bring the tor opposite into focus. Landscapes had always challenged her. She could never bring land and sky to life with a depth of field that captured the atmosphere.

Spider taking its prey. The secret lives of scorpions. Lioness saving her cubs. No problem. But despite what others said, she knew her landscapes always missed something. The grey clouds and flat light today didn't help.

As dawn broke this morning she'd slept fitfully in the armchair in front of the fire. Her dreams were fraught with an invisible force chasing her. The ghost of the past, present or future? She couldn't decide.

One thing was certain—she'd have to go to the police now. Until last night she still hadn't decided what to do about the note, but with the vandalism on the car, her mind was made up. Plus she was certain the hire company would insist upon it, which would force her hand anyway.

She whipped her head around at the sound of footsteps behind her.

"I thought I might find you up here."

She let out a sigh. She'd come up on the moor as an escape, to clear her mind and get her equilibrium back. Here she was trying to forget about everything, and the biggest reminder of all turned up.

"Not working?"

Devlin raised his mouth in a half smile. "My hours are rarely fixed."

"You?"

She lifted the camera. "Always."

He sat down next to her and leant forward, resting his elbows on the worn knees of his jeans. After studying the panoramic view for a few moments he turned his head towards her.

Her gaze fell to the tanned vee of his neck and the tantalising curl of chest hair peeking out. For one second she wondered what it would feel like to press her lips against it.

"I've often wondered when you started taking pictures."

His words startled her out of her fantasies and she shut down her train of thought, blaming it on the lack of sleep.

"Last couple of years of school. I joined the photography club, and the rest, as they say, is history."

If she was honest, she'd only started it as a way to avoid having to go straight home. But by the end of the first term she'd become addicted. Not just because it was easier to hide behind the camera, but she loved the sense of fulfilment she got from exploring her creative side.

Devlin sat back against the rock behind him. "Could you work closer to home?"

Jesus. Did he ever give up? She threw him a glare and he raised his hands in a defensive motion.

"I'm not trying to start another argument. I'm genuinely interested." He ran a hand through his hair. "I promised your dad I'd look out for you, but I seem to be screwing it up at every turn."

She gave a slight shake of her head, unsure whether he was apologising or about to pressurise her again. "I'm not eleven and walking to the bus stop alone any more, Dev."

"I can see that."

Something in the inflection of his voice warmed her in a way she refused to acknowledge.

"I just think you'll regret letting the house go."

She'd been thinking the same thing since she calmed down after the meeting at the solicitors, but there was no way she was going to admit that now. Besides, after last night she wasn't sure if she wanted to stay.

"One of the advantages to working freelance is that I can pick and choose my assignments. But if I limit my work to comply with Dad's ridiculous demands, it might hurt me in the future. There's no guarantee that I'll get offered some of the prize jobs I do now."

He leant closer to her. "So you enjoy going deep into the Amazon rainforest just to photograph a frog?"

Her brow drew downwards. *He'd noticed?* She didn't imagine any-one had ever looked out for her work. Well, except her dad. But that was what dads did, wasn't it?

"A frog no one has ever caught on camera before. Yes. Could I have done without seeing the destruction we're bringing, myself included, and knowing that its habitat would soon be gone? Absolutely." She smiled, realising how ridiculous she sounded.

"I sometimes think that way about the army. I love the opportunities it gave me, could have done without seeing humanity at its worse."

"But there must have been times when you felt you were making a difference."

He gave her a lopsided grin. "Always the romantic. Yeah. There were moments."

But not enough to obliterate the horrors. His tone said it all. She stared out at the horizon. In the distance she could see the red warning flags flapping in the breeze, a signal everyone knew meant the moor was off-limits while the military carried out manoeuvres. "Did you train on those ranges?"

He followed her line of sight. "Sometimes. I remember thinking how cool it was going to be, after all those years we used to look across and wonder what went on when the red flags went up."

"Did it live up to expectations?"

Devlin exhaled deeply. "Not really. It doesn't matter that it's live ammo in training, nothing prepares you for hostile engagement in real life."

They both stared out across the moors, lost in their own thoughts. She'd forgotten how easy it was to be in Dev's company. His stillness had always soothed her when she was younger.

"How did you know I'd be up here?"

"Mum said she saw you on the path. 'Walking up a storm' were her exact words."

Damn. She'd forgotten that in going out the back way and avoiding having to look at the car this morning, she'd be easily seen from his parents' farm.

"More like blowing the cobwebs away. I didn't sleep well last night."

"The wind's calmed down a lot this morning."

She hummed her response, hoping he'd leave at that and presume she'd been upset about her father, but his next words choked her.

"I spoke to my contact in the police."

She turned towards him. The compassion in his gaze filled her gut with dread. He knew.

He gave a dismissive shrug. "Maybe he just had a couple of beers and went for a drive. Stupid, but not unheard of round here."

She had to put an end to this and come clean. There was no way she'd be able to keep it quiet any more.

Chapter Eleven

"Stop." Grace leapt to her feet.

Devlin didn't need to look at her face to know he'd said the wrong thing. Her distressed tone was enough.

She stormed across to the edge of the ridge and then paused, with her back to him, breathing deeply as if weighing up her options. "I don't know what Dad told you, or why the hell he made the will as it is, but it was no surprise to me that he was over the limit when he had the accident."

Eventually she turned, the humiliation in her eyes pained him. "I was just grateful that no one else was involved."

His chest tightened. "I'm not sure I understand."

A heavy sigh escaped her. "Why do you think your mum got you to walk me to the bus stop all those years? She was probably one of the few people who saw him for what he was—a lost, confused, functioning alcoholic. Just because he wasn't in the pub, was always polite and would do anything for anyone, doesn't make it any less true."

Devlin thought back to his encounters with Geoff and realised she was right. Shit. He'd never seen it. Too young when he left for the army to notice, and too engrossed in his own demons when he'd returned.

He ran a hand through his hair. "I'm sorry, Grace."

Sorry he hadn't seen it before. Sorry for being such a hard-arse on her for not caring. And sorry he hadn't given her the sympathy she deserved from day one of her return. Regardless of her father. He was supposed to be her friend.

She swung back around towards the moor. "Don't beat yourself up about it, Devlin."

Her words cut through him. It was like she could read his mind, but he still couldn't figure out what was going through hers. Except that he was a dick. That was a given. He gave a slight shake of his head. "But I never even realised."

"You saw what he wanted you to see. I got the other side." She lifted her palms and gave a helpless gesture. It cut him harder still. He got up and walked over to where she stood.

"Did he hurt you?" he asked quietly, dreading the answer.

She peered up at him, her expression softening as she saw his concern. "Don't fret, Dev. He wasn't a mean drunk. Things just didn't get done. He'd do his work and then fall asleep in the chair beside the fire, leaving me to keep up the pretence that we lived a normal life."

He raised his hand to tuck a stray lock of hair behind her ear. "Is that why you left?"

Her eyes never strayed from the horizon. She was still clearly warring with herself about telling him the truth and betraying the memory of her dad. He waited patiently. Eventually, she started to speak.

"Going to university in London provided me with an escape I jumped at. I wanted to leave here and lead a normal life. Not have to cover for him." A derisory laugh forced its way out of her. "Although by the looks of it, maybe I was just enabling him all those years instead of helping. He obviously did a pretty good number on everyone after I left."

He swallowed. "Why didn't you come back?"

"If Dad wanted me to come home, he had to give it up. He knew that's what it would take, but he chose the bottle over his daughter."

His words the other day about her not being around for her father came back to haunt him and he let out a low curse.

She gave him a sideways glance, her eyes shimmering with unshed tears. He reached out and splayed his fingers across her jaw, turning her head to meet his gaze, her lips just inches from his. "I wish you'd told me."

"By the time it came to a head, you were gone." Her expression held a mixture of acceptance and regret. He didn't know which affected him most.

She moved away from his caress, and reluctantly, he released his hold. "What happened?"

She took a moment before speaking. "We argued about me using the car to go to a party. He refused, saying I'd get drunk and crash it. Looking back, I'd probably bottled everything up and it all came pouring out that day. We both said mean things."

"And there was no going back?"

She sighed. "Why is it when you're young everything is so black and white?"

He twisted his mouth in a grimace. "Life hasn't had a chance to get complicated."

Her brow furrowed, and she darted him a questioning look as she continued talking. "In the end, I gave him an ultimatum. If he didn't give up drinking, then I wasn't coming back after I left for university. We talked regularly, and he always knew how to get in touch with me, but I stuck to my word and never came home."

He tucked his hands in his pockets to stop himself from touching her again and stared down at the ground. "Why didn't you say something before?"

"Because you were the one piece of normality in my life. You didn't pity me because my mum had died. You didn't walk around on eggshells, unsure what to say. And you listened to me talk *endlessly* about animals."

He gave a half-smile at the humour in her voice. "I thought you were going to be a vet."

She groaned. "So did I, until I found out how much science it required. I really don't have the brain for that."

"I wished you'd let me help you."

He raised his head and caught her hazel eyes widened a fraction at his low tone.

"I didn't want your help."

He breathed in and exhaled deeply. "I mean now."

Her nose screwed up, as if she was undecided.

A sharp pain hit him in the chest. He'd thrown away the trust she once gave implicitly. "I know we've been at odds since you returned, but can't we start over, without all this bullshit between us?"

She gave a slight shake of her head. "You don't want to do that. If you start helping me, then you'll end up facing the village ire. Someone's already made it pretty clear they don't want me here."

"Fuck what people think. Who's said what now?" He loved Huntersford Leigh, but occasionally its residents could be small-minded and vicious.

She grimaced. "It's not so much what they said, but what they've done. Worrying about Dad wasn't the only thing that stopped me from sleeping last night. Someone decided to give my car a makeover and told me to stay away."

Devlin's jaw clenched. "They did what?" If he ever found out who it was, he'd tear them off a strip.

"Scratched the side of the car and wrote a message in the dirt on the glass."

His gaze narrowed. "Same as the note you won't show me?"

A blush hit her cheeks. "No. It was different. I think I interrupted them. The shed door was banging in the wind and I went outside to close it."

An uneasy feeling settled in his stomach. He wasn't about to tell her now, but his contact said they were still investigating her father's death, which implied there was more to it than a simple drink-driving incident.

He grasped her by the top of her arms and turned her to face him. "Next time, don't go outside. Call me."

She stepped back and broke his hold. "I'm a big girl, Devlin. I've been looking after myself in far more dangerous places than Huntersford. It's probably just someone who has some petty grievance."

"Have you contacted the police?"

She looked skywards. "I'm sure they've got better things to do. I just want to get everything sorted and get out of here as quickly, and with as little fuss, as possible."

The woman infuriated him. One minute he wanted to kiss her, the next he wanted to shake some sense into her. He wished she'd stop talking about leaving. In every conversation he'd had with Geoff, he'd clearly wanted her to come back to Huntersford Leigh.

Or maybe he hadn't. What the fuck did he know? He hadn't even spotted the guy was an alcoholic. Maybe he wanted Grace to stay away, and that's why he'd made the will as it was. He had to have known it would infuriate her.

"You could contest the will, you know. There must be some sort of 'not of sound mind' clause."

"That's just the problem. I think he was." She shrugged. "They were his wishes. I might not understand them, but I can respect them. He respected my wish to stay away." She ran a finger underneath the necklace around her neck. "I just wish I understood why."

Unable to resist any longer, he offered up the comfort he should have given her that first evening, and pulled her into a hug. She stiffened at first, and then relaxed into him.

Over the top of her head he watched the clouds racing across the sky, their billowing shapes casting dark shadows on the valley below. Eventually, he lowered his head, and whispered against her temple. "A person can get lost or go mad looking for a reason."

She leant back a little and looked at him. "You sound like you're speaking from experience."

His mouth tipped up a fraction. "Spent a lot of time in the dessert wondering just that sort of thing."

"Did you find an answer?"

He lifted his head again towards the moor. "Maybe. I'm still deciding."

The temperature had started to drop. In his embrace, Grace shivered. She looked pale and tired, and guilt ate him up that he'd been partly responsible.

"Come on. I'll walk down with you and take a look at the car." He stepped away, grasping her hand, and tugged her back towards the main path, grabbing her camera bag on the way.

Grace's heart raced as she closed the front door behind them. It wasn't the steep walk down or the bracing wind that took her breath away. It was the man whose broad frame filled up the hallway as he removed his jacket and slid off his boots.

She'd wanted to melt into his embrace up on the tor. To soak up the warmth and security she felt in his arms. It was the first time she'd considered that the pull of desire between them might not be one-sided. Maybe if she'd confronted him earlier with her fears, they wouldn't have been at odds these last few days.

On the way down, he seemed to take every opportunity to touch her, helping her over the rocky terrain to make sure she didn't lose her footing. And she'd accepted his hand willingly, even though she didn't need it. Had he been trying to shut down his attraction to her, too?

"And?" Devlin's voice was calm as he helped her out of her coat, but the tone had a steely edge. One that brooked no argument.

He'd already taken a look at the hire car and was now expecting to see the note, but she was still reticent to show him. Once he saw it, there'd be no going back to pretending it didn't exist. Even though that hadn't worked as a strategy either, since she thought about it constantly.

If only she understood what the letter was about, it would make everything so much easier. Wouldn't it?

"Grace?"

She huffed out a sigh and made her way into the living room. "I found it in the writing desk. I don't know when Dad got it, or if it even means anything at all. I wasn't going to mention it because it's his private life, but..."

She turned and handed him the envelope. He took it carefully, turning it over to examine it before pulling out the note.

His jaw clenched as he read it. "Do you have any idea what it refers to?"

"None. And I can't believe that Dad wouldn't own up if he'd done something dreadful."

"Were you going to tell the police?"

The way he questioned her, while keeping his expression blank, Grace couldn't help but think of Jess' comment in the pub. *What does Devlin say he does for a living?* "No. Maybe. I don't know."

He raised a brow and she threw up her hands. "What does it matter? He's dead. It was an accident." Her gaze drifted to the note. "Or at least the police think it was."

"But you don't?"

"The most surprising thing to me about the accident is that he had one at all. He might have been way over the limit, but that was nothing for him." She frowned. "Why?"

He paused for a moment. "That's what I came to tell you. My contact says they're still investigating."

A cold chill came over her despite the heat from the wood burner. "What does that mean?"

"I've no idea. He wouldn't go into details. But this," he placed the note back on the wooden writing desk, "might be far more relevant than you think."

He pulled his mobile out of his back pocket and tapped at the screen. "I'll send him a text and ask him to get in touch."

Grace opened her mouth to protest, but Devlin held up a hand.

"No. Let him deal with it and decide whether it's relevant or not. At the same time, he can take a look at your car."

Chapter Twelve

Devlin sat down in the armchair by the fire, grateful that Grace hadn't put up too much of a fight about getting Jared involved.

While she was out of the room putting the kettle on, he'd had another look at the note. He didn't want to alarm her, but with everything that had happened so far, it was all starting to add up to more than a coincidence.

But what the hell could Geoff have done? He agreed with Grace that Geoff would own up to any mistake he made, regardless of the consequences. So why would anyone accuse him of killing someone?

He went to stand as Grace walked into the room carrying a tray with two mugs of tea and a packet of Hobnobs.

"No. Stay where you are, it's fine." She placed the tray on the table and handed him a mug. "Help yourself to a biscuit."

They both sat back and drank their tea, lost in thought. After a while, he became aware that Grace was looking at him.

He eyed her cautiously. "What?"

"You're so intense."

He frowned. "And you're not. What happened to the kid that thought about everything so hard and long?"

"I learned to let go. There isn't time to reflect in photography. Plan, yes, but when the shot's there, you have to take it."

She got up to take their cups back out to the kitchen, and as he rose to help her, his phone beeped.

He scanned the message. "Jared can't make it until tomorrow. I'll stay the night, just in case whoever it was comes back."

"You don't have to do that."

He reached for her hands. Touching her soothed something inside of him in a way he couldn't even begin to explain. Nor did he want to explore it. She wasn't staying, and if he went back into the field, there wouldn't be much time for anything else.

"Grace, let me help you." He recognised the reluctance in her eyes, but he also saw relief there. "I'll feel happier knowing you're not alone, too."

She sucked in a deep breath and let go of it slowly. "Okay. But you should know I haven't cleared out Dad's room yet."

He studied the ageing settee behind him. "The couch is fine. I've slept in worse places."

The small smile she gave in return radiated heat into his heart. "Thanks, Dev. It would make me feel better."

Her agreement was a small victory, but he'd take it.

"I just need to go back to my place to grab a few things. I'll bring back a pillow and blanket so you don't need to worry about anything." He was also going to relay the information to Jamie and see if he could do some digging. But he didn't tell her that. No point in scaring her more than necessary.

"Can I cook you dinner in return?"

"Sounds perfect." He almost leant forward and kissed her on the mouth to seal the deal, without thinking. He caught himself at the last minute, leaving an awkward silence between them.

She bent her head and tucked a lock of hair behind her ear, muttering about checking the contents of her fridge, and turned to walk out of the room at the same time as he did.

He stepped aside and winked, trying to brush off what seemed like mutual embarrassment, before stretching out his arm. "Ladies first."

She raised her eyes heavenward. "Always the gentleman."

He watched the sway of her hips as she walked through the doorway and into the kitchen, and smiled to himself as his thoughts took an entirely ungentlemanly turn.

The bedside clock came into focus. A quarter to two. Grace had been staring up at the ceiling for the best part of two hours. Mostly thinking about Devlin.

Their uneasy truce had lasted through dinner and most of the evening watching TV. It wasn't until she stood to go to bed, and he brought up the meeting with Jared tomorrow, that the tension running between them surfaced again. Especially after she mentioned the feeling of being watched on the moor.

Perhaps a cup of tea would help her sleep. If she shut the kitchen door, hopefully she wouldn't disturb him. Sliding out of bed, she threw on her old dressing gown and crept down the stairs, careful to avoid the creaky tread three steps from the bottom.

As she crossed the hallway, her mouth went dry. Dev was asleep on the sofa, the blanket thrown back, revealing his naked chest softly lit by the embers of the fire. Her gaze roamed over his body, memorizing every inch, from the way his torso dipped down to his abs to lower still where the blanket lay tantalisingly across him.

A draft hit the back of her neck, causing a shiver to run down her spine. She pulled the collar of her dressing gown up, but the instant feeling of comfort was followed by a twinge of guilt.

He'd be freezing by the morning without a cover over him. She should be pulling the blanket up, not drooling over him.

Trying to be as quiet as possible, she walked across to the couch and gently tugged at the blanket.

His hand caught her forearm. "Leave it, Grace. I'm fine."

She glanced at him. Eyes closed, his face as impassive as always, she could have almost believed he was still asleep, if his low voice and strong grip hadn't sent shock waves of awareness through her body.

"But you'll be cold."

"I'm okay."

She huffed out a breath. "The temperature really drops once the fire's gone out."

"Are you offering to warm me up?"

Her breath hitched. *No.* She ogled his chest. *Maybe.*

As if he could sense her indecisiveness, his eyes opened. The glint of anticipation she saw there sent heat pooling low within her.

"Go back to bed, Grace."

His thumb rubbed over the sensitive skin of the inside of her wrist and her heart hammered in her chest.

"I will just as soon as you let me cover you."

"No." His grip tightened, pulling her hand away from the blanket.

"Why not?"

A groan emanated from his chest. "Because I'm holding onto my control by a thread not to pull you down to join me here on the couch."

Her jaw dropped slightly. Was it bad of her to wish he didn't have so much discipline?

His grip on her arm loosened, and she felt bereft at the loss of the warmth of his touch. But one look at his unmistakable hunger and every sensible thought she had in her head disappeared in a wave of lust.

"Control's overrated." She barely recognised her own voice, thickened by desire.

His grip tightened once more and he tipped her off balance, pulling her effortlessly over the length of his body. His palm cupped the back of her head, his fingers twisted in her hair, and he captured her lips in a searing kiss that blotted out all the reasons she shouldn't be doing this.

She opened her mouth to him, and he kissed her long and deep, like he was savouring his favourite treat. His tongue sliding warm and hot against hers stole her breath away.

Eventually his possessive claim on her mouth lessened and she drew back a little. She breathed in the scent of him. Warm. Spicy. Masculine. Her sanity returned a little. "Wow. Who knew you were such a good kisser, Devlin Judge."

She bent her head and placed a kiss on his neck.

Devlin turned his head towards her. "You have no idea how much I've thought about kissing you, from the moment you crashed into me that first night. My hands went out to stop you from falling and I never wanted to let go."

His rough whisper against her temple sent sparks shooting through her body.

"And there I was thinking you still thought I was that gawky kid from long ago."

"You were never gawky."

She lifted her head and stared at him, raising her eyebrows in disbelief.

He gave a half smile. "Okay maybe you were. But you had an inner strength I admired. You still do and you're most definitely not gawky now."

He stretched up and slanted his mouth over hers, and she lost herself to his kisses once more. She could feel the thick, hard ridge of his cock beneath her and wiggled her hips against him to increase the sensations building within her.

She ran her fingers over the broad shoulders she'd admired from afar. When she felt the ridge of a long jagged scar, she broke the kiss and moved to press her lips against the roughened skin, unwilling to think of the pain he must have endured.

No longer holding her head captive while he kissed her, his hands roamed over her back and slid underneath her pyjama bottoms. His fingers squeezed her cheeks and pulled her harder against his cock. She shifted slightly to her knees to increase the pressure and let out a low moan.

His fingers paused in their exploration. "Grace, we need to slow down."

She let out a groan of frustration. "Why?"

He placed a hand under her jaw, forcing her to look at him. "I'd like nothing more than to peel you out of your..." His gaze roamed over her as if noticing the pattern on her night attire for the first time, the ghost of a smile crossed his face. "Pink unicorn dressing gown, and taste every inch of you. But then I'd feel like that sleazeball guy who manipulates women by holding something over them."

"I'd never think that of you."

"Good." He leant in and kissed her hard on the lips. "Cause I'm not that guy. Now get what you came down for and go back upstairs before we both do something we regret."

Before she could protest, Devlin had her back on her feet and facing the doorway. A slight push on the small of her back had her taking a step forwards. She twisted around. He was sat up now, the blanket still covering his lower half.

The steely look in his eyes said there was no changing his mind. Not tonight, anyway. Maybe it was for the best. With a soft sigh, she bade him goodnight and walked out of the room, only pausing for a moment when his low, sexy voice muttering "sweet dreams" reached her ears.

Dreams? She'd be lucky to sleep at all.

Devlin inwardly groaned as he watched Grace suck the butter from her fingers one by one, before picking up her mug of tea and taking a sip.

The sound of a car arriving outside, signalling Jared's arrival, was just the distraction he needed. Especially since all he could think about was hauling her across the kitchen table and acting on several of the fantasies he'd been having over dinner last night. Not to mention those after she went to bed the second time. Even the thought of the unicorn dressing gown hadn't cooled his ardour.

But he wasn't going to act on any of it until things were more sorted between them. They might have ripped right through the just friends marker, but taking things further now was only going to make life messier. For the both of them.

He stood. "I'll get it."

She slammed down her mug hurriedly and rose from her chair. "No way. You don't know who it is. I don't need you answering my door at this time of the morning. You don't know what they'll think."

He placed a hand on her shoulder to stop her from rushing to the door. "You're forgetting someone is bound to have noticed my car outside all night and already drawn their own conclusions."

Her eyes widened with horror. "Oh."

He shrugged. "They'll think two people shared a fabulous night of amazing sex, and if they had any sense, they'd be envious."

"But we didn't…" she squeaked.

With a smile, he kissed the crumbs of buttered toast from her lips. "But we might have." Pushing her back towards her breakfast, he walked into the hall. "Trust me. It's Jared."

He opened the front door and shook Jared's hand. "Thanks for coming, mate." Glancing over at the constable standing just to one side, he turned back to Jared. "So this is official?"

"'Fraid so."

The woman stepped forward. "PC Brown, sir. DC Endacott suggested I accompany him."

He shook her outstretched hand. Grace was going to freak when she realised. But he was more glad than ever that he'd called in Jared. Obviously, they were no longer treating Geoff's death as a simple accident, and it was always better to look as if you were at least trying to co-operate with the police.

Stepping outside, he pulled the door closed behind him. "Okay. I'll show you the car, and then we can go in and chat to Grace."

He led the way around to the side of the house. Jared studied the car for a moment before turning to Devlin. "She interrupted someone, you say?"

"Grace thinks so. She didn't really see anything. She just came out to shut the shed door."

PC Brown studied the finger writing in the dirt for a moment before looking up. "Any guesses as to the full message?"

Devlin shrugged. "I presumed here?"

"Or him. You upset anyone recently, Dev? Jealous lovers?" Jared asked.

Shit. Him being here probably looked exactly like what Grace had been afraid of. "No. No one to be jealous. I stayed over last night in case they came back."

Jared's brow creased. "Okay. Let's see what Miss Vaughan has to say."

Grace was in the living room when they returned to the house. She greeted Jared and the constable with a smile when he made the introductions, but flashed Devlin a perplexed expression when she turned her back on them before taking a seat opposite the policewoman.

"I didn't expect two of you. I hope I haven't put you to any trouble?" Grace sounded casual, but there was an edge of wariness in her voice.

Jared gave her a perfunctory smile. "No, not all. There have been a few developments."

A frown crossed Grace's face. Devlin wished she had sat on the sofa so he could sit with her to offer moral support, but predictably she'd taken the single armchair.

He switched his focus to Jared who was studying Grace closely, as if trying to judge her motives from her body language alone. An unsettling silence filled the room.

Eventually Jared leant forward. "It appears your father's crash might not be the accident we first thought."

Grace visibly paled. "What are you saying?"

"We believe that someone deliberately tampered with the brakes."

Chapter Thirteen

Grace sat there, stupefied. Eventually, she found her voice. "Are you sure?"

"The Collision Investigation Team is quite certain. You seem shocked."

Grace raised her eyebrows. "Did you think I wouldn't be?"

The detective paused a moment. "The sergeant you spoke to before had the impression you suspected something was wrong with your father's death."

Pinpricks hit the back of her neck as Devlin's gaze swivelled towards her. She took a deep breath to give herself time to choose her words. "I was confused about the accident."

"In what way?"

It was no use. The police weren't going to give up. "I couldn't figure out how someone who knew a road like the back of his hand, who was used to driving having had a few drinks, could end up wrapping themselves around a tree."

"It's often all too easy." His tone spoke of too many traffic accidents.

"Yes. I get that. But no one else was likely to have been on the road, not in winter and not at that time of night. If there had been a deer or a pony, he'd have had time to take evasive action. It just didn't make sense." Or at least not until she found out his brakes didn't work.

"We're thinking alcohol was a contributing factor." The detective's tone was patient, like he thought it needed explaining to her, even though they'd made it perfectly clear already.

She pressed her lips together to stop herself from saying anything rash. "I realise that, but as I already said, he was no stranger to drinking and driving."

He kept his expression schooled, but the slight downturn at the edges of his mouth spoke volumes about what he really thought. Grace straightened her shoulders. She'd better get used to being judged, because this was only the beginning.

"Have you any idea why he was on Leigh Road?"

A muscle in her jaw twitched. "No. That's something else that doesn't make sense. Anyone around here would tell you they avoid it. Full of tourists in the summer, flooded or icy in winter. At night he'd normally be asleep in that chair over by the fire." She lifted her chin towards the chair she'd slept in herself the other night.

She could picture him there now staring into the flames of the wood burner, a glass of whiskey beside him, while she sat on the sofa watching television. She'd often find him still there in the morning and had taken to wrapping a blanket around him when she went up to bed.

"Can you think of anyone that would have something against your father?"

The detective's question jarred her back to the present. She was starting to go dizzy with all the questions. "No. He got on with most people."

He tilted his head. "Just not you?"

Her jaw clenched. "We got on fine, so long as we stuck to the phone."

He made some notes before looking back up at her. "I understand you found a letter?"

Oh yes, the letter. She'd been trying to blot it out of her mind. Wasn't it bad enough that everyone would find out he was an alcoholic? Now they would all know he probably killed someone, too. Bang went any hope of her pretending to people like the Weird Sisters that her dad was a kind, if slightly misguided man.

She got up and went to the writing cabinet, returning to hand the envelope to the detective. Was Devlin sure this guy was a friend? He didn't seem it.

"And you know nothing about this?" he asked, giving the note a cursory look.

"I'd never seen it before, until I found it a few days ago."

"But you didn't think to tell us?"

"I'd been told my father's death was an accident. I didn't see the relevance."

He passed the letter to the constable. "What was your relationship like with your father?"

Grace sat back down. "Strained. We argued a few years ago, and I left."

"What was the argument about?"

She curled her arms around her middle. Answering honestly seemed like a betrayal of her father, even though it was true. "His drinking." The words came out as a mumble.

"I'm sorry, I didn't catch that."

She looked up, meeting the detective's stare head-on. "His drinking," she said more clearly, before looking away again. The detective waited for her to continue. "It started after my mother died and grew steadily worse. Not so bad that he couldn't hold down a job. He never got into fights. There was always money if I need new clothes or something."

She found herself defending him, and grimaced at the irony.

"So you left and never came back?"

He made it sound so dramatic. In reality, it was just fortuitous circumstances on her part.

She shrugged a shoulder. "I left to go to university in London."

"When was the last time you spoke to your father?"

"A couple of weeks ago. I was on assignment in Australia and knew it would be difficult to get a hold of me for a few days. I wanted to let him know."

He rubbed his brow with his pen. "So despite your estrangement with your father, you still let him know where you were."

She blew out a breath. "I said our relationship was strained, not estranged."

"Was there a will?"

She groaned inwardly. Everyone was going to know every sordid detail of her life by the time this was over. "Why?"

She'd watched enough cop shows to know the answer. She was just delaying the inevitable.

"Answer the question, please."

"Yes."

"Are you the beneficiary?"

She wrinkled her nose in distaste. "Sort of. There are conditions." She glanced at Devlin. He looked calm, but the clench of his jaw gave away that his silence so far was at breaking point.

They thought she'd killed her father to get to her inheritance? What a joke. She wasn't hanging around long enough for that. Not before. Definitely not now.

"Did you know about the conditions before your father's death?"

She slumped back against the armchair cushions. Damn. She hadn't thought of that one. "You can check with the airline. I was in Australia."

"We will, thank you. Did you know about the conditions?"

Devlin rose from his chair. "Jared, can I have a word?" He gestured to the door.

"Sure."

As soon as they left the room, the constable started going through her notes, confirming details. Grace tried hard to hear what was being said, but they'd moved into the kitchen and all she could distinguish were low voices, not words.

A couple of minutes later, they came back into the room, the detective not even waiting until he'd sat down to start questioning her again. "We can see from your father's bank account that money, in addition to his salary, went into his current account. What can you tell us about that?"

As if they didn't know it came from her.

"I don't have a regular income, so I'd just send him money when I had some."

"To a father you never saw?"

"Yes." Now she was getting pissed off with the line of questioning. "Contrary to what half of this village believes, I am a good daughter." A lump caught in her throat. "Was," she corrected herself.

"And who thinks you're not?"

It took all her willpower not to look in Dev's direction. "It was a figurative turn of speech. I couldn't actually name anyone. I've barely been back a week."

"Still time enough for someone to feel the need to put scratches on your car."

He let the statement just hang there, and Grace cursed him silently.

"You think that's separate from the note and Geoff's death?" Devlin interjected.

The detective frowned a little. "Could be. There's been a spate of burglaries recently. Maybe someone thought the place would be empty and got vindictive when they found it wasn't. We'll know more once we conclude our investigation."

He stood up and held out his hand. "Thank you for your time, Miss Vaughan. Don't go anywhere. We'll be in touch."

Devlin walked back into the living room after seeing Jared and the constable out of the house. His gaze immediately fell to Grace, sat in the armchair, her eyes closed.

She was so still he could almost imagine that she was asleep, but for the lines that creased her forehead.

"Sorry."

Her eyes flew open as his low voice carried across the room. They glistened with unshed tears and his guilt ratcheted up a notch. He hated to see her like this.

"What on earth do you have to be sorry about?"

Gesturing towards the front door, he gave a dismissive shrug. "I thought he'd be more sympathetic."

Her mouth twisted into a wry smile. "He's just doing his job. You know as well as I do that it must have been someone Dad knew. The faster they rule us out, the quicker they can concentrate on finding the real culprit."

"Yeah, but you were in Australia."

She raised a brow. "I could have hired a hitman."

"As if." He sat down opposite her.

"I can't believe it. I mean, I know I questioned the accident, but to hear that someone deliberately did something to his car..." She placed her chin on her palm and stared at the flames in the fire. The frown on her face grew deeper.

"So if it's not Jared's enthusiastic questioning, what are you beating yourself up about?"

She sighed. "I feel guilty."

He couldn't possibly imagine what for. From where he sat, it sounded more and more like Geoff was the one who owed Grace an apology. Not that she was ever going to get one now. "But you had nothing to do with your father's death."

Her lips twitched with playful amusement. "Thanks for the vote of confidence. No. I mean, I feel guilty because I was relieved."

That he hadn't been expecting. "Why?"

"When Detective Endacott first said the brakes had been tampered with, all I could think was thank god I didn't have to tell anyone about the drinking." She fidgeted with her fingers in her lap. "I realise that it's all going to come out anyway. But I'm just feeling bad about thinking it in the first place."

Devlin shook his head. "You're in shock, Grace. You're not a bad person."

She let out a mock snort of laughter. "Someone told me recently I failed as a daughter."

"Yeah. Well, that guy is an arsehole. I'd tell him to fuck off if I was you."

She smiled and stood. "I might just do that."

As she moved past him, he reached out and grasped her hand, pausing her progress. "Seriously, Grace. Your dad wouldn't want you to worry about what other people thought."

"No. He never did."

She stiffened under his touch and Devlin frowned at the hint of regret in her tone, but he let it pass. She had enough going on without him questioning her every thought.

He stood up and followed her over to the writing desk. "Come stay with me for a few days."

She folded up the flap and turned the key, reaching up to place it on the shelf above. "No. I'm not letting someone snooping around at night chase me off."

"That might not be the best decision."

"What?" She turned, fire lit her eyes. And, sick fuck that he was, he took a perverse delight that he'd put the passion back into them. Anything was better than the slightly lost look that was there before.

She took a step towards him and poked him in the chest. "You've been telling me at every opportunity that I should be fulfilling my father's last wishes. Am I going to look up the board of directors for the pony charity and find your name there?"

"What? No, of course not." He grasped her finger. "Think about it, Grace. If someone tampered with his brakes, where did they do it? Outside the house has to be the most obvious place."

Her eyes widened. Now he was annoyed with himself. He hadn't meant to scare her.

"Who would do such a thing?" she stuttered, almost to herself.

He pulled her close and brushed her hair away from her face, framing her cheek with his palm. "I don't know. There are some crazy people out there."

She pushed against him, fear set aside and determination in its place. "Well, there's a crazy person in here too, if you think I'm staying with you and feeding the village gossip mill."

"Rumour mill."

She punched his arm.

"*Ow*. At least go stay with Jess."

Her expression sobered up. "No. I might put her in danger too."

"Then stay with me. If the fucker comes after you, then at least I've got a rifle."

Her face paled and he ran a hand down her cheek. "Sorry. I didn't mean to scare you, but you need to take this seriously. It's not just about your dad. Someone's been back here since he died. Maybe the two incidents aren't connected, but at least give the police a few days to see where their enquiries go."

He could see her determination wavering. "You can still come back here during the day to sort things out." Not alone, but he didn't need to mention that right now. "And I promise if it goes on longer than a couple of weeks, I won't say a thing."

She rolled her eyes. "The length of time doesn't matter. I've told you I'm not staying."

He pushed aside the twinge of disappointment her words caused. "Then there's no reason to refuse my offer."

She pursed her lips. "There are plenty of reasons to refuse you, Devlin Judge, but maybe, just this one time, you're right. I should stay with you. Just for a couple of nights."

He thought about getting her to repeat that he was right, but even he knew when not to push his luck. He was just content that for the time being, she was staying. With Grace, he'd take the wins when he could get them.

Chapter Fourteen

G race fidgeted as Devlin unlocked his oak front door. She was already regretting her decision. Regardless of whether or not she'd actually be safe staying at the cottage by herself, staying with Devlin was dangerous for entirely different reasons.

She peered up at his broad shoulders. They'd felt so good underneath her fingertips last night. Taught, strong muscles that rippled beneath his warm skin. Grace gave herself a mental shake and forced herself to look away.

By the time she had her wayward thoughts under control, Devlin was already inside, placing her large camera case next to the hall table.

He glanced back at her, a frown creasing his brow. "What are you waiting for?"

She grimaced. "I don't want to put you to any trouble."

"We've been over this," he said as he straightened up. "I wouldn't have offered if I didn't mean it."

But he hadn't offered. He'd demanded. She took a deep breath and stepped over the threshold. Maybe now wasn't the time to split hairs. "Thank you."

"You're welcome." His gaze captured hers. A mixture of empathy, anticipation, and desire swirled in the steel-grey depths.

It was a heady combination. Especially after that kiss last night. But, as much as she hated to admit it, Devlin had been right to bring their make-out session to a halt. Life was complicated enough right now without giving into attraction just to satisfy her libido.

Reluctantly, she broke off the connection. She had a vague recollection of her dad saying Devlin had bought the old barn on the other side of the village. At the time she'd imagined something dark and depressing, but the open-plan space in front of her was a welcoming mixture of wood, metal, and brick flanked on one side by enormous windows.

"Wow. This is amazing."

Devlin walked over to the living room area. "Thank you. I had planned to do a lot of the work myself, but I never had the time. In the end, I hired a contractor from Bovey."

"They've done a fabulous job."

"Yeah. I was lucky. I particularly like how they made the most of the old barn opening and the views." He nodded towards the glass wall in the living area that presumably was used by horses and haycarts in years gone by. "Go, take a look."

She wandered over while he went back out to the car, pausing to look at a couple of photos in frames on a shelf. One was a school photo of the nine of them with Mrs Hargreaves. Judging by their age, it must have been taken just before Devlin and Jamie left for senior school. The other was Devlin in his army uniform, somewhere hot and dusty, surrounded by teammates.

She continued over to the window. From the barn's high vantage point, she could see right across the village and up the hill opposite to where Devlin's parents lived at Moors Cottage Farm. She craned her neck to see if her dad's cottage was visible, but a clump of trees obscured the view.

She turned as Devlin came back into the house and closed the door. "I'm seriously jealous. The view is amazing."

He grinned. "It's pretty special, isn't it? Not as good as sitting up with your back against a tor, but a lot warmer in winter. Come on, I'll show you the guest room and get you settled."

At his indication, she followed him across the living area and through a door beyond.

"I think you should have everything you need, but let me know if you want anything else." He placed her bag next to the bed.

A twang of disappointment hit her chest, and she chided herself. Only a few minutes ago she'd been convincing herself that she was right not to follow through on their growing attraction. But she rarely listened to her sensible side.

She peered at the bed and then back at Devlin, raising her eyebrows just a fraction.

"I'm trying not to be the sleazy guy, remember?"

She twisted her mouth into a half-hearted smile. "Always the gentleman."

He took a step closer, reached out, and tucked a lock of hair behind her ear. "I wouldn't go that far. I'm more than interested in showing you the master bedroom. I just figured I'd give you the choice."

Her breath hitched. Now would be the time to let him know that she was interested too, but with everything that had happened today her cautious side won out.

As good as his word, Devlin barely missed a beat as he carried on to fill the silence. "You have your own bathroom through that door there."

"Thanks, Dev." She meant about letting her stay, but with the pulsating atmosphere between them, it might just as well have meant about him giving her space.

He responded with a tight smile. "My pleasure. I'll give you some time to settle in."

"Oh, I forgot." She saw the hopeful glint in his eyes and rushed on before either one of them said something stupid. "A letter for your mum was mixed up in the post today. Can you give it to her?"

"Yes, of course." He took it from her and flipped it over taking in the address. "Must be a replacement postman. Thanks."

He tapped the envelope against his palm as if he wanted to say more, and she prayed that he didn't question her further. The last thing she wanted to do right now was examine what had happened between them. Though how long she could put it off, given that she was staying with him was questionable. *Like the rest of your behaviour,* she mentally berated herself.

He turned to walk out the door, then paused. "I'll go see what I've got in the fridge for dinner. Or we could go to the pub if you prefer?"

She screwed up her nose. "Would you mind if we stayed in? I know I'm not going to be able to keep me staying with you a secret in this village, but after today with the police and everything, I just want to get my head straight before I have to face a barrage of questions."

"Sure, no problem. And Grace?"

"Yes?" Her heart hit her throat as she caught his gaze. The desire she'd seen in his eyes last night was back in full force and the effect was hypnotic, spine-tingling, and oh so dangerous.

"No one has to know that you're sleeping anywhere other than in my spare room, if that's what you want."

Unable to meet his intense regard any longer, she cast her eyes down towards the wooden floorboards. Her throat was dry, her breasts heavy, and a warm heat pooled low in her centre. She was sorely tempted to step forward and make the first move. But the courage of last night had fled with the morning light and all she could do was mumble a pathetic thanks.

She looked up as he reached for the door handle, and he winked, making her heart skip a beat. In that simple expression, she was transported to those days long ago when he used to cajole her out of her misery over the death of her mother and make her laugh again. Usually at his expense.

"Come out when you're ready." He pulled the door closed behind him and she sank onto the bed.

Had she really just turned down an invitation from the guy she'd spent the rest of last night fantasising about?

She ran her hands over the crisp bed linen and frowned. Somehow she couldn't imagine Devlin picking out the abstract floral pattern. Had some other woman chosen it for him?

Her dad had never mentioned anyone in Devlin's life, but then again, it was highly likely that he wouldn't have thought it important enough to tell her.

She dismissed the jealous thought as the bruised ego of her teenage self. She had no claim to Devlin, especially if she had no plans to stay in Huntersford Leigh. She stared down at the covers again. *But still.* The thought of someone else making personal decisions about the decor of his home irked her.

Pushing herself off the bed, she stood and started to unpack her meagre things. Taking her toiletries into the bathroom, she was struck by the heavy wall grips beside the bath and in the shower. Had Devlin used this room when he was recovering from whatever gave him the scar she saw last night?

She let out a frustrated sigh. It was strange having once known someone so well, and now not knowing them at all.

Maybe Jess was right. Leave the past behind.

Devlin pulled salad ingredients out of fridge and started to slice lettuce, determined not to think about the way Grace had responded to his offer of showing her his room.

Had he scared her off by mentioning it? He hoped not. But he understood her reticence. She'd been on a roller coaster ever since she arrived back at Huntersford Leigh and he hadn't exactly rolled out the red carpet, even though he'd felt the attraction from day one.

The door from the guest room opened, but he didn't need to hear it to know Grace was near. Ever since she returned, he'd had a heightened sense of awareness whenever she was around.

With half an eye still on the food he was chopping, he watched her as she sauntered across the room. It agitated him that he couldn't stop his body reacting every time she was near, as much as it pleased him to see her reflect that same level of attraction. Well, at least some of the time. Judging by the worry lines marring her forehead, currently, not so much.

By the time she'd reached the counter, the frown was gone, replaced by a forced lightness in her face and her tone. "Can I do anything to help?"

He wondered how much she always hid of herself. Not for the first time in the last few days, it crossed his mind that he'd misjudged her completely. It wasn't that she didn't care. It was that she cared too much. Didn't want others to worry about her.

But now it was all he could do. That, and imagine what it would be like without the death and distrust between them. He forced his thoughts out of the gutter and responded to her offer of help. "Sure. Can you fill that pan with water, please? If it's okay with you, I've got lamb chops under the grill. And I thought we could have them with salad and fresh pasta?"

"Sounds great."

He nodded towards the wine rack. "Feel free to choose a bottle of wine and open it. The glasses are in the cupboard up above."

She filled the saucepan and set it on the stove. "Did you want a glass?"

"Just a small one. I need to work later."

The frown returned. "I'm sorry, Dev. I didn't think. Are you sure it's okay for me to stay here?"

He put down the knife and turned to where she stood, removing the bottle from her hand and placing it down on the counter. "Absolutely."

He reached up to cup her jaw. Giving in to temptation, he leaned in and kissed her. As he pulled away his adrenalin jumped as her cheeks pinkened. "There's no way I want you staying anywhere else while some idiot is running around out there looking for trouble."

"I don't want to be a burden."

Her words weren't just platitudes. She genuinely thought she was a pest. A small smile reached his mouth. He wasn't about to tell her that, in fact, he was secretly very pleased to have her in his home. "You're not. I mean that."

The corners of her eyes crinkled in appreciation, and for the first time since she'd returned, she seemed genuinely relaxed. "Thank you, and thanks for helping with the police today."

He released her and went back to preparing the salad before he did something he'd regret. "I didn't do anything special."

She sighed. "You probably stopped me from making myself look more guilty than they already think I am."

He frowned. "I'm sure they don't think you're a suspect."

"Really? Even after he asked me to stay and make myself available?" The cork popped as she pulled on the corkscrew.

"Standard procedure. I'll have a word with Jared if you like." He glanced up as she began to pour the wine. Her brow had creased back into that frown he'd been working so hard to rid her of.

"You can do that?"

"What's the point in having friends in high places if you can't take advantage once in a while?"

She gave him a saccharine smile as she passed him a glass of wine. "Well, if I'd known that, I'd have committed two murders instead of one."

He flashed her a grin, knowing exactly who would be the second victim. "But if you'd done that, who would have run interference with the police?"

"True." She raised her glass. "Cheers. And again, thank you. Talking to them was like walking through customs."

Their glasses clinked as he raised his. "Customs?"

"You know, all those officers in uniform staring at you intimidatingly. Always makes me behave guiltily because I go out of my way to act how I think *they'll* think is normal."

He laughed at the madness of her statement.

She raised her eyebrows at his disbelief. "I'm serious. Had you not been there today, I'd have been ridiculous in my attempts to prove it couldn't possibly be me, and made myself look more guilty."

"How often do you get stopped at customs?"

"It's different when I'm working because I always declare all my gear, but I think my name must get flagged up when I'm travelling for myself, because I frequently get stopped."

"That sounds like a pain."

They worked in companionable silence for a few minutes, the sound of soft rock on the speakers filling any awkward silence. Devlin checked the chops and tipped pasta into the boiling water, while she set the dining room table and took over their glasses of wine.

As if by unspoken agreement, they kept the conversation light during dinner. Grace told him about some of the countries she'd worked in and he tried to avoid most of her questions about his work, beyond where he'd served.

"And now you work for Agema?"

"Yes."

"Weren't they all cloak and dagger when we were kids?"

He gave her a lopsided smile. He had to give her points for trying different tacks. "They still are."

"Ah. Which is why you're being so secretive."

"I prefer the term evasive."

Her gaze narrowed. "Can you say what you do?"

"Cyber-intelligence."

The corner of her mouth lifted. "Which covers just about a hundred and one different jobs."

"It keeps me busy."

"What does Jamie do?" Picking up her glass, she took a sip of wine.

"I don't know."

She clamped her hand to her mouth as she tried to swallow the wine without spitting it out. Maybe he needed to up his small talk.

Clearing her throat, she glared at him. "Seriously? You expect me to believe that?"

"It's true," he said, passing her a napkin. "I've a pretty good idea. But he's in another division, and it's beyond my pay grade."

Her equilibrium regained, she stood and picked up their plates. "I don't believe a word of it, Devlin Judge, but I'm smart enough to know that you wouldn't do anything to jeopardise those around you."

He closed his eyes momentarily as she turned towards the kitchen. She couldn't know how her words sliced him in two. She had blind faith in him, and yet that was exactly what he had done. Missed a crucial piece of evidence and wiped out an entire operation, along with Ronnie's life.

Chapter Fifteen

Grace closed the dishwasher and turned to see Devlin walk over to the couch with their wineglasses. He looked more sombre than he had a few minutes ago. Had she inadvertently said something out of turn? She'd only been teasing him about work.

Growing up in an area dominated by the military, she was all too aware of how little they gave away. A slight smile lifted her mouth. Even the warning notices in the local paper of upcoming training activities were vague. They were only issued after someone complained about being frightened by the helicopters at night.

She and Jess had often wondered who won that battle. The pair of them used to imagine the fun someone had writing those notices, which appeared as if they were being considerate to residents while saying absolutely nothing at all. She still couldn't imagine why anyone would complain. She'd always marvelled at the pilots' skill when they'd hear two helicopters running close together, but only ever see the one with its lights on.

Turning out the kitchen light, she joined Devlin on the couch, taking the seat furthest from him. Twisting round to face him, she tucked her sock-clad feet under her and reached for her wine.

With the curtains drawn against the cold and the darkness, the only light was the flicker of flames from the wood burner and a dimmed table lamp behind the sofa. She took a sip of her wine before resting her head on the cushion.

"Penny for them?"

She frowned. "What really bothers me is, if it wasn't either of us, then who was it?"

"And why?" Devlin placed his legs up on the coffee table.

Their long length distracted her as she remembered how strong they'd felt beneath hers last night.

She forced her gaze upwards to meet his. "I have a horrible feeling that damned note is the why. But I still can't believe it's true, any more than I could when I first found it. Up until today I could convince myself that reading anything else into it was just grief and an over-active imagination."

"You're far too sensible for that."

Was she? Until she came back to Huntersford Leigh, she'd thought so too. But now she was thinking about throwing away her carefully planned life to have a few nights of hot sex with the man in charge of her father's will, while trying to figure out just who killed him in the first place.

And maybe, just maybe, staying. At least for a year, just to see what happened.

Of course, knowing that one of her fellow residents might be a murderer did put a dampener on the whole thing.

"Suppose it was someone in the village? It could be any one of those people in the pub last week who offered me condolences." An involuntary spasm shuddered down her back.

Devlin gave a slight shake of his head. "It seems unlikely."

"None of us are the same people we were before. You were right the other day, some things are still the same. But like the river that flows through the village, its path changes over time. People too."

"But murder? I just can't see it."

She stared down at her hands. The last couple of weeks had taken their toll. The revelation by the police today was the final straw, and a bone deep tiredness dragged her down. "We both know that evil has a way of touching beauty when we least expect it. I was reminded of that today when I looked at the photo of us all together on your shelf."

"She was such a beautiful person. It hardly seems fair."

Devlin's low voice held a hint of regret, as if something could have been done to save Katie. But the truth was that no one could have foreseen what happened.

She wiped away a stray tear that rolled down her cheek. "There was never any hint of anything wrong when I spoke to Dad over the last few months. I've thought about relatives we haven't seen in years. Gone through everyone he knew locally. It just doesn't make any sense. Is it possible Dad didn't know them?"

"No. It wasn't just some random fight outside a pub. The brakes make it planned. Unlikely for a total stranger."

She raised her head and met Devlin's gaze. "Who would want him dead?"

He reached out and brushed his thumb over her cheek, cupping her jaw with his fingers. "I don't know. We just have to trust that the police will figure it out."

She tilted her head towards the warmth and comfort his hand offered. His grip tightened and despite the fatigue of a few minutes ago, a spike of awareness charged through her body. She turned her head and kissed his palm.

His groan, followed by him whispering her name, was all the encouragement she needed to know Devlin craved this as much as her.

She rose to her knees as his hand slid around to the back of her head, pulling her towards him. She breathed in the intoxicating male scent of him, mixed with the hint of cologne rising from the warmth of his skin as she drew close.

Their lips met in a crushing kiss, and as she opened her mouth his tongue swept inside of her, cajoling and teasing her senses into a hot, quivering mess.

His lips slid from hers and he continued a trail of kisses down her neck before nibbling the lobe of her ear, sending delicious pinpricks of shivers across her body.

"I keep telling myself to keep my distance, Grace. But every time I see the same hunger in your eyes, I lose a little of my self-control."

His kisses continued across her shoulders and trailed along the valley of her cleavage until his mouth found the pointed tip it was searching for.

She clasped the back of his head with her fingers, gripping him tighter as he kissed her nipple through her blouse. "Don't stop on my account."

Devlin's hand slid underneath her legs, and eased her onto her back, flat against the couch. His body was warm as he followed her down onto the sofa, still nuzzling her breasts, and she arched her hips against his chest, craving more of what he had to offer.

The ache inside of her increased as he deftly undid the buttons of her blouse and pushed the silky material aside. His pupils widened as he regarded her lacy turquoise bra, making her thankful that she'd included a couple of pieces of sexy lingerie in her last shopping trip.

He teased her nipple out from behind the lace. His lips closed around the taut, erect flesh he'd revealed and sucked hard, until she was lost on a wave of lust-fuelled desire. When his hand slid under her skirt, she gripped his shoulders tighter. She was trying to stay clear-headed, but failed miserably as he traced his finger over her panties and across her sex, leaving her moaning for more.

He raised his head. "You like this?" He ran his finger over her again and her internal muscles clenched.

"I'd like it more with you inside of me."

Her mouth went dry at his smouldering look. But before she could reach down to pull his shirt out from his jeans, he retreated. He replaced the lacy cup of her bra back to its position and sat up, his hand stroking down the length of her leg in a regretful gesture.

"Sorry. I didn't mean for us to get so carried away."

She took some comfort in hearing that his voice was rough with desire. He was right, of course. Following through on their obvious attraction to each other wasn't the wisest move given the circumstances. But right now, she was prepared to live with the consequences.

"I want you, Grace. Make no mistake about it. But with the conditions on the will, and now the police investigating your dad's death, I feel like I'm taking advantage. As if—"

She sat up and leant over, shushing him with her finger. "Stop. You're right. I'm not myself right now. I have more questions than answers, and I'm second guessing myself and my sanity every step of the way. But this..." She flicked her finger between the pair of them. "This isn't going away. So just remember, third time's the charm." As she stood up she bent over, knowing she was giving him an eyeful of what he was missing, and a small, petulant part of her felt good about it.

She placed her lips gently on his. "Sweet dreams."

And then she sashayed away to the guest room, hoping he was regretting his decision to stop as much as she was.

Devlin breathed in deeply. A run in the cold morning air was just what he need to clear his head. Not to mention working off some of his pent-up energy from having Grace constantly nearby.

He hadn't thought it through when he insisted Grace stay with him. While he wanted her safe and meant it when he said she could stay in the spare room, he hadn't realised how much it would test his self-control.

Halfway across the field that led from the bridle path to the village, he caught sight of Callum walking towards him with his dog. At least coming this way, he could kill two birds with one stone.

He slowed his pace as Callum approached, before turning to fall into step with them. "Hi. Mind if I walk with you and Daisy for a bit?"

"No. Course not." Callum gave him a sideways glance and then continued without missing a step.

Devlin had a feeling Callum was used to being ambushed by residents wanting a quiet chat while out on his morning walk. His suspicions were confirmed when Callum filled the silence with a possibly pre-emptive question, while Devlin was still thinking about how to broach the subject he wanted to talk about.

"How are the legs?"

"Much stronger than a few months ago. I never imagined it would take this long to get back to even a reasonable level of fitness and mobility. Still catches me by surprise every now and then."

"Injuries like that take time." Callum frowned and stopped Devlin with a hand on his forearm. "You're not trying to get back out in the field, are you?"

"Maybe. Hell, I don't know. I'm grateful for the job Jamie got me, but I'm not going to lie. I miss being at the cutting edge."

Callum shook his head. "Adrenalin junkies, the pair of you."

Devlin bent down to scratch Daisy's ear and the chocolate Labrador tipped her head into his hand. "I wanted to ask you a question."

"Fire away."

"How much alcohol can someone drink and still function normally?"

Callum switched Daisy's lead from one hand to the other and continued walking. "Depends. Several factors influence it. Sex and weight, obviously. Some evidence shows that other factors can also contribute, but I'd say it generally depends on how much they're used to it. Doesn't mean they can function normally as you're suggesting, but maybe it's not as obvious with some as it is with others."

They'd reached the stile at the end of the path. As Callum stepped over it, he paused. "Is your question to do with Geoff?"

Devlin looked up from where he'd been lifting the dog gate for Daisy. "Yes. You knew?"

Callum gave him a look of disbelief. "I'm the village doctor, of course I knew."

"The police think there's more to his death than an accident."

"Well, it wasn't suicide," he said, stepping off the stile. "He was too much of a stubborn, curmudgeonly old bastard to do that."

Devlin kept his voice low. He knew how sound travelled on a still morning like this. "No, it wasn't suicide."

Callum looked back at him sharply. "Christ."

"Keep it quiet for now, although once the police really start asking questions, it will be all over the local area in no time."

"What do they think happened?"

"Someone tampered with the brakes."

Callum frowned. "Now I feel mean for calling him a curmudgeonly old bastard. He was, but no one deserves that. Poor Grace."

He looked up at the cottage across the valley. "Is she safe up there?"

"She's staying at my place while the police carry out their investigations."

Callum raised his brow.

"Not like that. She's in the spare room." Much to his disappointment.

Callum just grunted and Devlin quashed down the niggle of annoyance at people judging what they knew nothing about.

But it didn't fool his friend. "I'm just saying you two always shared some sort of close friendship years ago." He shrugged. "It would make sense to pick up where you left off."

"We didn't have anything going on to pick up. Anyway, how come you don't date anymore?" It was a crass attempt to deflect the conversation away from being too close to the truth, but he didn't care if Callum saw through it.

"I'm a doctor in the middle of fucking nowhere, with fuckwits like you for patients. No offence meant." Callum let out a sigh. "Who the hell is ever going to be interested in me?"

Daisy licked his hand, and Devlin gave him a wry smile. "Well, someone loves you. Perhaps if your bedside manner improved, others would be too."

"You can go off people, you know." Daisy tugged at her lead, but Callum stayed where he was. "Does Grace have any idea what or who is involved?"

"Not a clue." He wasn't about to mention the letter. It wasn't that he didn't trust Callum. It was just the feeling that the letter held some kind of significance they hadn't figured out yet.

Callum's gaze had wandered back to the cottage. "I often wondered why she didn't come back in all those years. I tried talking to Geoff about it once, but he just brushed me off, saying she had to lead her own life and didn't need a broken man holding her back." His watch pinged. "I've got to go. Early surgery today. Thanks for the heads-up. If I hear anything, I'll let you know. Say hi to Grace for me."

As Devlin stepped out of Callum's way, his leg twinged. One thing was for certain, she didn't need another broken man holding her back. Maybe Grace was right that letting the house go would free her from the past.

He slipped off his sweatshirt and tied it around his waist before heading back up the path. Didn't stop him thinking what the future might hold though.

Chapter Sixteen

G race bit into her scone and groaned as the taste of jam mixed with thick clotted cream assaulted her taste buds. "Now this, I've missed."

She sipped her tea, before layering up the other half of the scone, ignoring Jess' look of mock horror.

"Don't let Mrs Hargreaves see you do it that way," Jess hissed across the table. "She'll think you're a traitor to the whole of Devon."

Grace gave her friend's comment the eye-roll it deserved. "I never understood why there was so much debate as to the right or wrong way. They're not on my plate long enough for anyone to care." She took another bite to prove her point.

"Mrs Hargreaves does." Jess' curls bobbed up and down with the movement of her head, just as they'd done when the pair of them had been six years old, sitting in the front row of the village school.

"Yes. But she also cares about the gnomes in her garden and growing ridiculously enormous vegetables. Neither point to someone I should take notice of."

Jess leant forward, her elbows on the table. "Yeah, but she did look after the house until you got here."

Grace smiled to herself as she remembered the key under the flowerpot. "I'm not saying she doesn't have everyone's best interests at heart, but sometimes it borders on intrusive."

"It's because she thinks we're still those cute little children she used to teach. To be honest, I've gotten so used to it I don't think I even notice anymore."

Jess poured out the last of their pot of tea and Grace sat back in her chair, staring out of the cafe window. The sky had darkened and rain threatened. There was talk of snow next week and her time in Australia seemed like a distant memory.

She'd spent most of yesterday trying to distract herself by editing some of the pictures she'd taken there before her trip had been cut short. But it didn't do any good. She couldn't silence the questions going around in her head.

It didn't help that Devlin wasn't there to distract her, either. He'd gone into work and then called to say he wouldn't be back until late. She suspected he might be avoiding her, but she was grateful for the breathing space.

She pressed her lips into a thin line. Her friends had changed since they were at primary school, just as she had, and with all the new people who'd arrived in the village she no longer knew who to trust. She glanced over at Jess, checking her phone for the millionth time to see if she'd sold any of her jewellery online while they'd been out, and smiled.

At least she still had Jess. They'd picked up their friendship as if she'd never been away, and Grace was grateful. Especially since she probably didn't deserve it, having never been one for keeping in touch at the best of times. "Thank you for coming with me."

Jess looked up and offered her a small smile. They'd spent the last hour finalising the funeral arrangements. "I'm surprised Dev didn't want to come."

Grace wrinkled her nose. "What was it I said the other day? Still think they're in charge?"

Jess flashed Grace a look of understanding before going back to her phone.

Devlin had wanted to come, but Grace insisted that she'd already arranged to have Jess with her. It was awkward enough over the will. The last thing she needed was him commenting about her choices for Dad's funeral.

Since her car had been locked up in his garage and the funeral directors had a car park, she'd persuaded him she'd be perfectly safe. No one would, or could, tamper with her car. It was just too surreal to think that anyone would want to in the first place.

It didn't make any sense. She could hardly believe anyone would want to harm her father, so why on earth would anyone seek her out?

Far more probable was the detective's assessment that someone thought the house was empty and her intruder was the culprit behind the series of recent break-ins in nearby villages.

After the meeting with the funeral directors, she and Jess had decided they needed a pick-me-up treat and walked the short distance to a high street cafe, leaving the car in the safety of the private car park.

She looked over at Jess and sighed. It was all going to come out soon enough, and if Jess heard about it on the grapevine she'd be hurt that Grace hadn't confided in her.

"There's more."

Jess put her phone down on the table, her gaze alight with mischief. "I knew it."

Grace rolled her eyes. "I haven't told you what it is yet."

She wasn't ready to confess everything just yet, but Jess' over-active imagination was already going there.

"You don't need to. Devlin's always been protective of you."

"No. It's something else. I didn't get those scratches on the car by driving too close to the hedgerow…"

Jess' jaw dropped further and further as Grace told her everything from her father's will to visit from the police.

"And they have no idea who it might be?"

Grace shrugged. "If they do, they aren't saying anything."

Jess sat back in her chair. For once she seemed speechless.

"And Devlin is the executor?" she finally asked.

"Yes."

Jess frowned. "Are you sure he's not just luring you out of the house so he can get it? Though I have to admit that doesn't sound like Devlin."

"He doesn't get a thing, the ponies do. But I'm only staying with him for a few days. As much as I still can't make sense as to why someone would hurt Dad, Devlin does have a point, especially with someone snooping around outside the other night."

Jess rested her hands on the table and asked quietly, "And he hasn't made a move on you?"

Grace's hesitation was her downfall, and Jess pounced on it. "See, told you. Though it does make it deliciously interesting that he's the executor."

Grace stifled a groan. She was never going to live this down. "Come on, let's go back home."

As they left Exeter and took the road leading to Huntersford Leigh, Grace picked up speed. The rain was falling steadily now, and the traffic was starting to thin. The rear lights of a slow-moving car ahead of them came up fast.

The road was straight and she could easily see in front, so she clicked on the indicator and pulled out across the lane to overtake, speeding up again once she passed the other car.

As she moved back into her lane a flash of light caught her eye, and she looked in the rear-view mirror. The headlights of another car overtaking the same vehicle glared back.

She focused on the road ahead. The rain was starting to come down heavier, and she gripped the wheel a little more firmly as she concentrated on the road.

Suddenly, the bright lights of a main beam reflected in the rear-view mirror, blinding her for a moment. She raised her hand to shadow the glare. "I hate it when people do that. If they're going to overtake, why not wait until they've already moved out before turning on their main beam?"

The car approached them rapidly, and she adjusted her speed to let them overtake. If they were going to drive inconsiderately, she'd rather lose them, and fast.

At the first jolt, she let out a short cry of surprise as the steering wheel jerked beneath her hands. "What the fuck. Did they just clip us?"

Jess turned in her seat to look behind them. "They've pulled back. Maybe they're stopping." She swung around again. "There's a layby up ahead. We can pull over there. Hopefully, they'll—"

The second jolt was harder than the first. Grace eyeballed the rear-view mirror. "They're backing up again. Do I speed up or stop?"

"Here's the layby, pull over. If they pull in behind, floor it."

Grace pulled sharply to the left. A dark SUV drove past at speed.

Jess' phone lit up the car's dark interior as she fumbled to press the buttons. Her hands were shaking as much as Grace's.

"Who are you calling?"

Grace could hear the person on the other end clearly ask what service was required. Jess proceeded to explain that they'd been in an accident and the other driver had driven off.

"What are you doing?" Grace implored Jess.

Her friend gave her a stupefied look as she covered the phone's mic with her hand. "They might come back."

Grace took a deep breath. She hoped not.

Jess finished up the call, and half turned to Grace. "Someone should be here soon. We don't know how bad the damage is and I'm not getting out of this car." She started to scroll through her contacts again.

"Who are you calling now?"

"Devlin."

"No, Jess, he doesn't need to be involved."

"He gave me very clear instructions this morning. Anything out of the ordinary happens, I call him. I don't care if that was just some nutter who can't drive. I'm definitely classing it as out of the ordinary."

Grace sank back into her seat. At this rate the solicitor wouldn't need to worry about her leaving Huntersford Leigh for more than two weeks. He'd be lucky if she ever left the house again. Maybe she should just cut her losses, take the hint that someone was obviously giving her, and leave, permanently.

She barely registered Jess' conversation with Devlin. Her focus was glued to the road in front of her. Every time headlights appeared, she held her breath until the vehicle passed without incident.

Only when the familiar blues and twos came into sight did she allow herself to relax.

Devlin pulled out of the layby, leaving the police loading Grace's car onto a trailer. Thank god Jess had called him. He was convinced that if he hadn't been there, Grace would never have told the police about her father's crash.

He pressed a button on the steering wheel and moments later, Jamie's voice came over the car's speakers. "Yo."

"Grace has been run off the road."

"Shit."

Grace tilted her head towards the mic to be heard more clearly. "I wasn't run off the road. I pulled over."

Devlin shot her a sideways glance. "The car's a wreck. They hit her up the back a couple of times."

"Whereabouts?"

"About fifteen minutes out of Exeter. I'm sending you the coordinates."

"You okay, Grace?" Jamie's voice softened and a spike of jealousy hit Devlin, even though it was nothing more than a friendly, concerned enquiry.

"Yeah. Jess and I are fine. Just a bit shaken."

"Jess was with you?"

Devlin relaxed slightly. Apparently, Jamie's concerned voice for Grace was nothing compared to his tone for Jess.

Jess leant forward from the rear seats. "I'm here now. Don't get too excited. You still owe me ten quid for our team beating yours last week. Nothing short of death will stop me collecting."

Jamie paused for a moment. "Sure you're okay?"

"Yeah. Don't worry about me. Find out who this bastard is that's trying to scare Grace."

"That's what I'm phoning about," Devlin interrupted. "Grace says she didn't see anything unusual until she and Jess were out on the open road, so I'm guessing they picked her up as she came out of Exeter. Can you get someone to check out the CCTV? They were parked at the funeral directors and then headed out around five."

"On it. I'll get back to you as soon as I have something."

"Thanks. The police are going to look into it, but you know it will take time to go through the official channels."

"What's happened to the car?"

"Police have it, just in case it ties in with—" Devlin stopped. Grace didn't need to hear him and Jamie discuss her dad's death in plain facts.

For them, it was like any other operation they'd work on. Set emotion aside and get on with it. But although she had more colour than when he'd first arrived, Grace was still pale and clearly shaken up.

"Okay. I'll see what they're willing to share."

Jamie hung up and the three of them continued in silence to Huntersford Leigh.

They let Jess out in the centre of the village and waited until the light shone in the loft space above her workshop. A few minutes later, Devlin pulled into his garage and shut off the engine.

Aside from saying goodbye to Jess and eliciting a promise that she'd call if she was worried about something, Grace hadn't said a word most of the way home.

He snuck a look across at her now. In the glow of the garage lamp lamps she reminded him of the lost girl she'd been years ago, wide eyes glistening with tears against pale porcelain skin that made him want to reach out and haul her into his arms.

Except she held herself so stiffly, he was afraid he'd break the control she had a tight rein on.

"Do you think they ran Dad off the road?" Her voice was almost monotone, and he knew she was picturing her father going through a similar episode to what she'd been through tonight.

He reached over and laid his hand over hers. It was icy cold. "No. The damage to his car was all at the front, whereas yours is crumpled at the rear."

A cold wave of fear had washed over him when he realised how fast the other vehicle must have been travelling. She and Jess were lucky to have escaped without injury, although he suspected they'd both be feeling bruised and sprained once the adrenalin wore off.

He squeezed her hands. "Come on. Let's go inside and get you warmed up."

Chapter Seventeen

As the warmth and security of Devlin's home encompassed Grace, the paralysing shock of the last few hours began to dissipate. Frustration and annoyance at her inability to fight back against an unknown threat took its place.

There was no denying someone had killed her father and was now targeting her. But who the hell was it? Had it even started that second day back in the car park?

A chill rippled across her shoulders as she removed her coat and placed it on the edge of the bed. Did that mean someone had been waiting for her to return to Huntersford Leigh?

Her fists tightened as she walked back into the living room. Regardless of the will, or what the police had to say, one thing was certain. As soon as her father's funeral was over she was high-tailing it out of here.

"Tea, wine, or something stronger?"

Devlin's voice broke through her train of thought.

"Stronger. Brandy, if you've got it."

He was standing in the kitchen looking every part the highly trained operative she suspected him to be. Alert. Disciplined. Formidable. And with a body she longed to touch.

He lifted his chin towards the sofa. "Go take a seat and I'll bring it over."

Grace scanned the living area. She was too worked up to sit. Sitting would mean brooding, and she was fed up with the thoughts spiralling out of control in her head. If it had been daylight out, she'd have grabbed her camera and gone onto the moor to take pictures and give her brain something else to focus on. But it wasn't. It was dark and someone was gunning for her. And despite everything, she wasn't stupid.

Besides, she'd never get past Devlin. Jess had accused him and Jamie of always muscling in where they weren't needed, but she'd been glad of it today. Before she'd even thought of mentioning her father's crash to the police, he'd been on the phone to Jared, bringing the detective up to speed.

Of course, it would probably mean another interview like the other day, which she wasn't looking forward to, but maybe they'd be one step closer to finding her father's killer.

She watched as Devlin reached up to grab a bottle of Remy from one cupboard and a glass from another, his muscles outlined to perfection through the tight black t-shirt he wore. Her mouth watered remembering the way her fingers had roamed over them on the couch the other night.

What she needed was a distraction.

She walked around the kitchen island and wrapped her arms around Devlin's waist, pressing her front to his back, and kissed the nape of his neck. "I don't want to sit."

His shoulders stiffened. He paused for a second before turning around in her embrace and clasping her upper arms, pushing gently to create a space between their bodies. "It's just the adrenalin wearing off."

If it wasn't for the gleam of desire she saw in his expression, she might have backed off. Instead, she rose onto her toes to meet his gaze head on. "I know you're doing this to protect me. But I don't need the nice guy tonight. I need you."

A smile tugged at his lips, regret filling his eyes. "I'm still the nice guy."

She nudged him in the ribs. "Didn't anyone tell you nice guys finish last? Live a little."

He stared straight ahead at the wall behind her. She could sense his indecision. Her heart skipped a beat as he slid her a guarded look. "Grace, if I pass my physical, I'm going back in the field. I can't make you any promises."

"I'm not looking for promises, just a moment to forget. Besides, I have nothing to offer either, with my nomadic lifestyle."

"Your dad's given you a chance to change that."

She placed her fingers over his mouth to silence him. "Not now. I don't want to think. I just want to feel."

She searched his face, looking for a sign that he was relenting. Desire was still there, but so was that core of steel that ran through his bones. Sex crossed a line they couldn't take back, and she understood his reticence, but it didn't stop her from hoping.

She inched her feet closer to his. "What do you have to lose? If we regret it, we probably won't see each other for another decade anyway."

An inexplicable moment of melancholy washed over her, but before she could dissect the emotion, Devlin hauled her to him.

As he scatted kisses across her jawline and down her neck, his rough voice and five o'clock shadow tickled her sensitive skin. "Grace, you'd test the willpower of a saint."

She turned her head to claim his lips with hers, and as if a dam had been broken, he took charge. Coaxing her mouth open with insistent kisses, his tongue swept over hers and tangled around it in an erotic dance. She placed a hand on his chest to steady herself. The strong thump of his heart beating beneath her palm sent a thrill through her as she realised he was just as affected by their kiss.

Arching herself towards the rigid length of his shaft, her mind went blank as she gave herself up to the sensual onslaught his kisses induced. Her toes curled, her thighs tingled, and a rush of heat swept through her.

She ground her pelvis harder against him until he groaned and broke them apart. She was afraid he'd changed his mind about pursuing the attraction between them, but instead he spun her around, grasped her hips and lifted her onto the island counter. Stepping between her thighs, he cupped the back of her head and pulled her in for another searing kiss.

Her pulse jumped as he trailed his other hand up underneath her top and caressed her nipples beneath her bra. Every part of her body tingled with awareness, but desire still gnawed at her. She needed to feel his hard muscles and warm skin beneath her fingertips.

Tugging at the bottom of his shirt, she pulled it out from the waistband of his jeans. Not content with exploring the bare skin she'd revealed, she dipped her fingers below his belt hoping for a tantalising touch of the velvet steel she could feel beneath the rough material. But he grabbed her wrists, pulling her arms above her head, and gently pushed her back on the kitchen worktop.

"I won't be the nice guy if you carry on like that."

Grace's mouth slid upwards into a smile as the double meaning behind his words registered. Devlin was tempted to lean over and kiss the sexy smirk from her lips, but she was too delectable spread out on the countertop like a midnight feast.

His dick hardened as his gaze roamed over her. The blouse she wore, already half open from the buttons he'd undone, revealed a lacy bra with a tantalising glimpse of hard nipples poking through. He continued his exploration down her body, unfastening buttons as he went, exposing yet more tanned skin.

"Were you sunbathing topless in Australia?" He wasn't sure why the thought of it bothered him so much.

She raised an eyebrow. The flecks of gold in her hazel eyes seemed more vivid than before, giving the alluring promise of the erotic delights to come. The hint of amusement there told him his questioning was way out of line.

"I've got tan lines."

"And I can't wait to discover them." Bending down he scattered kisses along her centre line, ready to devour her the way he'd dreamed about over the last couple of weeks.

He undid her jeans and pulled them down her thighs, along with her panties.

Bending down, he blew gently across her silken folds and was rewarded by the trembling of her thighs. He swiped her clit with his tongue, and her muscles tightened. When he lifted her hips to angle her better against his mouth and sucked hard, she mewed like a kitten.

Sliding his hand over her body, he palmed her breast. The taut nipple beneath his fingers was evidence of how close she was to coming. Placing her back down on the countertop, he slowly inched first one, then two fingers inside of her, still caressing her swollen clit with his lips and tongue.

Her cry of release as she clenched around his fingers sent a spike of hot, intense desire through him. Continuing to kiss and stroke her core, he waited for her orgasmic haze to clear.

Then, after kissing her on the mouth one more time, he scooped her up into his arms and strode towards the stairs. Halfway up, it occurred to him that he didn't even feel a twinge in his legs. Was that the driving force of his desire, or did he really did have a chance of passing his physical?

Who cared? With Grace in his arms, her hot lips nibbling his neck, there was only one place he wanted to be right now, and that was inside of her.

He continued straight into his bedroom, placing her in the centre of his bed. Hooking his fingers into the neck of his t-shirt, he pulled it up and over his head before shoving his trousers and underpants down and kicking them to one side.

Grace was already sitting up on the bed. She reached for his cock, which was standing to attention against his belly, and curled her hand around it. He closed his eyes and gave himself over to the powerful waves of desire her slow, strong strokes evoked in him. When her lips engulfed his erection, he curled his hand around the back of her neck and encouraged her until he could stand it no more.

Then he pushed her gently back onto the bed, and continued where he'd left off previously, kissing her soft skin everywhere his mouth fell. He could see the wetness between her legs and craved to feel it sheathed around him. Reaching over to the bedside cabinet, he pulled out a condom and rolled it over his shaft.

Covering her body with his, he pushed himself up on his forearms and fixed her with a stare. "You sure about this?"

"I've never been so sure in my life. You'd better not be about to back out now."

He kissed her slowly. The taste of himself on her tongue only made his cock harder. "Wild Dartmoor ponies wouldn't stop me."

A faint smile crossed her lips at his pathetic attempt at a joke, and as she arched her hips towards him, he thrust inside of her.

He stilled for a moment, allowing her body to adjust to the size of him and giving himself time to absorb the rapture of being buried deep inside of her. As he began to move with a steady rhythm, she wrapped her legs around his waist, increasing the intensity of their intimate connection.

Her skin felt like softly woven silk beneath him as he pumped his hips. He lowered his head to capture her nipple, rolling his tongue around its erect form as her fingers twisted in his hair and she whimpered out her need for more.

He changed the angle of his pelvis to hit her clit with every thrust, heightening the growing tension between them. She moaned loudly as her inner muscles clenched around him and he claimed her mouth in a savage kiss, revelling in her orgasm pulsating down his cock.

As she relaxed, he upped the pace of his strokes, desire clouding his vision as he pounded into her sweet body. It wasn't long until his balls tightened, and her name was ripped from his lips as he poured out his own release.

For a moment, they both lay there breathing hard, their bodies covered in sweat. He bent his head and kissed her, savouring the sweet taste of her. "Sorry if I was too rough. I sort of lost control towards the end."

She raised her hand and cupped his jaw, the embers of the fire between them still glistening in her gaze. "I liked it. I never see Devlin Judge in any other mode but in control. I like that I can do that to you."

His chest tightened at the serene smile on her face as she spoke. But before he analysed the feeling too hard, he rolled over, disposed of the condom, and flipped her out from under him, delighting in the playful yelp that escaped her lips, before settling her on top of him.

With her thighs straddling his body. The warmth of her core pressed against his belly. And her lush breasts just begging to be kissed. He didn't want to be anywhere else but here with her. "If you like it that much, I'll let you do a whole lot more too."

He ducked out of the way as she tried to swat the side of his head.

A jolt behind her woke Grace up. She blinked a couple of times, pulling herself out of the deep sleep she'd been in. Her back was curled into Dev's side, but it felt damp. As she turned around, he shouted out something that sounded like *stop*.

Wide awake now, she shook his shoulder. His body was drenched in sweat. She moved her hand over his heart. It was thumping out a rapid tattoo. His arm jerked out, pushing her back into the mattress. She moved onto her knees to avoid being trapped and shook his arm.

"Dev. Devlin. Wake up."

His arm went stiff. His eyes opened, bright and alert, and he sat up as if ready for action. Then he met her gaze, and she saw the shock register on his face as he took in what must have happened.

He swung his legs over the side of the bed and sat up, his elbows on his knees and his head in his hands.

She hesitated, unsure what to do or say.

As her mind raced through her options, she figured it would be better to let him go at his own pace. She rested a hand on the small of his back, presuming that comfort was what he'd need more than words. Something to ground him in the real world.

Eventually, he eased back onto the bed, pushed the pillow up behind him and sat back. He lifted his arm, making a space for her, and she snuggled in, resting her head against his chest.

"Sorry." His voice was quiet, like the air of tranquillity that comes after a storm.

He reached over to brush a lock of hair away from her forehead and something about the gesture struck her as incongruous. It should be her offering comfort, not the other way around.

She'd already decided in those intervening moments that empty platitudes weren't going to cut it. It was one of the things she'd loved about her friendship with Devlin when they were young. He never asked her how she was coping, forcing her to respond as if her whole world hadn't just been turned upside down just to spare someone else's feelings.

She rested her hand over his ribs. His heart rate had slowed. His breathing was steady. "What happened?"

He remained silent and just as she thought he wasn't going to answer, he cleared his throat. "We walked into a trap."

His tone was flat, void of emotion, but it only served to emphasise how much had been lost. She waited for him to continue. "One of the team died. The others were lucky."

Her fingers traced the scar on his shoulder. She'd seen the much larger one on his leg last night too, when he'd taken off his trousers. "Except you."

"It was my fault."

Chapter Eighteen

Grace's breath caught in her throat. She didn't believe his words for a moment. It had to be the traumatic sense of loss talking. Devlin would never deliberately put anyone's life in unnecessary jeopardy.

"Is that what the report says?" She had no idea how the military operated, but there must have been some kind of assessment.

She felt him shake his head.

"They were wrong. My intelligence. My decision. My fault. I let my guard down and trusted someone when I should have known that something was up."

"How come?"

"It was too easy. We were gifted the intel we'd been waiting for, from a source we'd had reliable information from before. We just didn't know that this time his family was being threatened."

"Was it an explosion?"

"Right in front of me." He ran a hand through his hair. "I didn't get that gut feeling something wasn't right until we were close to the target. I was calling to Ronnie for her to fall back when the bomb blew…" His words drifted off and Grace sensed he was lost in his own guilt.

At the same time, a vague recollection of something her father mentioned fell into her mind. "Is that the incident where you were awarded a medal?"

He absently kissed her temple. "It doesn't matter what others say. I know I let Ronnie down that day."

She wanted to argue with him. To make him see that his point of view was skewed. But the nightmares, the injuries, and a death on his conscience weighed up heavily against the truth. She understood how survivor's guilt could overshadow the truth.

Instead of words, she pressed her lips to his chest to offer what solace she could.

After a while, she moved away slightly. "So you came back to Huntersford to recover?"

"I couldn't move around much to begin with. Dad arranged for the spare room to be adapted as I couldn't manage the stairs."

She pictured the heavy railings in the bath and knew she'd been right in her assumption. "And now?"

"Some days are better than others. But I'm hoping I'll pass the fitness test in a few weeks and be able to get out from the desk job I'm tied to at the moment."

Grace bowed her head. She might have been looking for a distraction earlier, but she was fooling herself if she wasn't hoping for more.

She lay back down under the covers. The grey light of dawn was filtering through and though the room was warm, her body was starting to cool.

Devlin followed her, pulling her into his arms, spooning her from behind. She wiggled back against him, and he hardened in response, nibbling the back of her neck and curling his hand around her breast. Nightmares temporarily forgotten, she gave herself up to the overriding desire building in her body.

Devlin stared at the flames in the wood burner as he sat on the sofa, legs stretched out, his feet resting on the coffee table. Grace lay on the couch pressed up against him, snuggled in the crook of his arm. A stillness had settled between them that was restful after the stresses of the day.

Jared had come round mid-morning to get a full statement from Grace before heading off to see Jess. And Grace had spoken to the hire car company, who were less than impressed that one of their cars was now in the police pound.

But sitting here, watching dusk fall on the moor through the picture windows, the sense of peacefulness was something he could get used to.

Grace had spent the afternoon on the terrace with her camera equipment, while he'd worked in his study. Every now and then, when he knew she wasn't aware of him, he leant back in his chair so he could watch her through the doorway.

He was fascinated by the speed and skill with which she changed up equipment and moved around to get the best light. Later on, when he heard her muttering to herself about her inadequacies as she reviewed the photos on her laptop, he stood behind her in awe.

If this was her worst work, as she professed, he'd couldn't wait to see her best. In her photos of the village, she'd captured the very essence of Huntersford Leigh. It reminded him of pictures that he would often evoke to help him through the long months on deployment.

Now she sat up on the sofa, squinting at the window. "It's a bit late for a bonfire, isn't it?"

Devlin leant forward to see what had caught her attention. His heart hit his throat. "No, that's my folk's place." He leapt up and grabbed his mobile, racing for the door. "Phone the fire brigade. I'm going over to help."

Grace almost ran into him as he paused at the front door to collect his keys. He turned to tell her to stay at the house, where she'd be safe, but her defiant stare said it all, even before she spoke.

"Don't argue, Dev. You know it will take a while for them to arrive. I can phone in the car."

Normally he'd argue, but they didn't have time. He nodded his agreement and they ran for the car.

He drove at break-neck speed into the village, ignoring the Please Drive Carefully sign. Grace had one hand on the grab handle and the other holding her mobile as she relayed the address to the operator. "Moors Cottage Farm, off of the main road into Huntersford Leigh. The flames are visible, they won't miss it."

The tyres squealed as he took the sharp bend up onto the moor road, past Geoff's cottage. His heart hammered in his chest as he took in the flames engulfing one half of the main barn. Parking beyond the farm to make sure there was room for the fire engines, he charged out of the car.

His mum was in the courtyard with a hose blasting water at the barn, but it wasn't enough to control the spread of the fire.

"Dad's inside trying to make sure all the sheep are out. Go, make sure he's okay," she shouted.

Grace ran past and started to set up a second hose further along, close to where thick black smoke billowed out the open barn door.

He covered his nose and mouth with his sweatshirt as he ran in. "Dad!" It wouldn't be long till it reached a point when smouldering stopped and the fire really got going. He realised now that it was lucky they'd seen it so early on.

"Over here," came back the shout. "Can't move Lucy."

Mum's favourite sheep. A few hundred roaming the moors and his mum could always pick out Lucy from a distance. Said it was her ears.

He turned the corner and found his father down beside the ewe. "Here, give me a hand. I don't like to hurry her, but she doesn't have time."

His dad pulled at two small legs just poking out of the sheep, and flopped the lamb onto the ground, clearing the membrane from its mouth. It lay there still for half a second before taking its first breath.

He immediately reached back. "There's a second."

Devlin straightened his back and look around. "We don't have long, Dad. Everyone else out?"

"Yeah, I opened the back doors and sent them out onto the moor. I'm just hoping it's only her about to give birth." He pulled out the second lamb. "Right. Grab those two and I'll make sure Lucy follows."

Devlin made his way out of the barn, holding the lambs up towards Lucy to encourage her to follow him. He'd done it enough times as a child to know the routine.

As they emerged, the fire brigade turned up, followed by the police. By the time he and his dad had penned Lucy in over the other side of the farmyard, the firemen were fully set up, leaving his mum and Grace looking on in dismay at the carnage the fire was wreaking.

They walked over to where a policeman and a firefighter were directing the operation.

The fireman turned their way as they approached. "What happened?"

His dad rubbed the back of his neck, an angry look on his soot-smudged face. "Crazy bastard. Was about to come out and check the ewes, when the dog started barking. I opened the door and saw someone around by the barn."

"Had the fire already started?"

"I didn't see it. I reached back in for my gun to fire off a couple shots to scare them, but they were already off down the lane and heading across the fields towards the village. Should have shot 'em in the back."

The policeman gave his dad a look, but said nothing. Devlin figured he'd heard it all before. The UK's strict firearms legislation meant that most people were limited to shotguns and rifles, which were supposed to be securely locked away. But the increase in rustling in recent years had made farmers a little less cautious of the law when it came to protecting their livelihoods.

"Must have started on the field side of the barn," his father continued. "By the time I got over to check out what they'd been doing, the fire already had a grip."

"Can you give a description of the person?" the policeman asked.

"No. Dark clothes, medium height. Could have been anyone."

The copper relayed the information back to base and went over to another officer to get him to search the local area. But they all knew the culprit would be long gone by now.

"Sit down, Anna, I'll get the tea. You look dead on your feet." Grace picked up the kettle, filled it from the tap and placed it on the Aga.

It had been nearly three hours since she and Devlin arrived at the farm. He was still out there now with his dad, trying to round up the sheep that had been released to escape the fire.

The firemen were packing up and there was just a sole police car out front.

The backdoor opened and the firefighter in charge of the crews stuck his head in.

At Anna's insistence, he came in, standing by the door so as not to muddy the kitchen floor. "Just finishing up. Thought you'd like to know our initial assessment. We don't think it was rustlers. Looks like it was started deliberately near where your husband first noticed the fire."

Anna's jaw fell as she adjusted to the news, and the hairs on the nape of Grace's neck rose. There was no way this was a coincidence.

What the fuck had happened to Huntersford Leigh? She'd imagined coming home to gossiping villagers, not someone hell-bent on murder and mayhem.

Anna collected herself enough to thank him and the other firefighters for their help. He refused her offer of tea, which Grace was grateful for. Anna's teapot only just held enough for four cups, so quite how she'd manage enough for two fire crews was beyond her.

He'd no sooner left than Devlin and Mick walked in through the door, toeing off their boots and hanging up their jackets on the pegs by the door.

"Tea! You're a saviour, Grace," Mick said as she passed him and Dev a mug.

"Did you talk to the fireman?" Anna asked.

"Yeah. Doesn't make sense. It definitely wasn't kids messing about. Who'd want to set fire to a barn full of sheep?"

Before anyone could answer, the doorbell peeled, and Anna rose to answer it. She returned a minute later. "This young man says he knows you, Devlin."

She stood to one side and Grace smothered a groan. The last person she wanted to see so soon was Detective Jared Endacott.

"Hi. I heard about the incident and thought I'd come out."

"Thanks, Jared." Devlin stepped forward to shake his hand.

Anna and Mick glanced at each other, and Grace realised that, of course, they'd no idea what had been going on. True to his word, Devlin hadn't said anything to anyone. They knew nothing about the will, her father's car, or the series of incidents that had befallen her.

"I was ready to stop at Miss Vaughan's, but then I saw all the lights up here. Any chance our attackers are confused about locations?"

"Wouldn't be the first." Piped up Anna. "Damned new postman still doesn't know the difference between Moors Cottage and Moors Cottage Farm."

Grace's breath caught in her throat. Her gaze locked with Devlin's and from the light of realisation in his eyes, his thoughts were the same as hers.

Just who exactly was the target?

Chapter Nineteen

Grace turned the key in the lock and opened the front door to the cottage. It seemed forever ago, that first night she'd arrived back, but had it really been only a couple of weeks?

She'd never imagined then that she'd end up in some kind of nightmare with Devlin as her protector. Although his surliness that first night was going to be nothing compared to when he found out she'd gone back to the house today without him.

But she couldn't wait. There was still too much to sort through and the weather was turning. The met office had issued a strong storm warning starting this afternoon and if she waited until Devlin returned from work, it might be too late and that would be another day wasted.

Besides, it was only one o'clock, and she planned to be here no more than an hour. Just enough time to organise some boxes and persuade Jess to come over and drive her back to Dev's with them.

The walk across the fields had helped clear her head. She was still desperately tired after last night, not to mention mortified that her father's actions had impacted on Anna and Mick. Her cheeks had blazed yesterday as Devlin explained to them exactly what had been going on.

And even though his parents had been really sweet and concerned for her, the sight of the burnt-out barn in the moonlight as they left filled her with contrition.

Devlin had left for an early morning meeting, but promised to be back this evening. He was convinced that they been looking at everything from the wrong angle. But though it had seemed a possibility last night, in the cold light of day, surrounded by the memories of growing up with her father, and the discovery of the note still fresh in her mind, she wasn't sure anymore.

She caught sight of the picture of her mother hanging on the wall, and her chest tightened. Maybe going through her dad's belongings without sitting in the cottage surrounded by memories would be less painful, too.

She walked up the stairs and turned left on the landing, crossing into her mum and dad's room. Funny how even though her mother had been gone for years, she still thought of it that way. Although, it was no surprise really, considering her father hadn't changed a thing in the intervening years.

Placing a cardboard box on the bed, she started to empty her mother's bedside cabinet. She forced herself not to look at the cards, diaries, and knick-knacks she uncovered. If she started that now, she'd lose track of time.

She cast a glance towards the window. Rain was already hitting against the windowpane and she turned on the bedside light to illuminate the darkening room.

Walking around the bed, she began to repeat the process on her father's side. Her breath caught as she opened the bedside drawer. Staring back at her was a white envelope with Gracie written in her father's scrawl across the front, two slanted lines underneath the end of her name. So familiar, and yet, she never expected to see it again.

A tear slid down her cheek. She pushed the box to one side and sat down on the bed, reaching for the envelope. It was unsealed. Her fingers moved of their own accord, pulling out the sheet of paper before she had a chance to think about it, her subconscious taking away the decision of whether to open it now or later.

Gracie,

If you're reading this then I guess I've joined your mother — hopefully she'll still have me!

Her lips twitched at her dad's characteristic dark humour.

I'd really like to think we would have made our peace before this happens, but who knows? We understand better than most how life can be taken at a moment's notice.

By now, you'll probably know about the will. I'm sure you're cursing me enough to fill the jar in the kitchen, but I hope one day you'll realise I did it out of love.

I drove you away from a community that cared for you more than they did me, and for that I'm sorry.

If you peek out from behind that camera one day, they will embrace you again.

Love you always

Dad x

Grace sniffed and ran a hand across her cheeks. She still didn't really understand why her father had made the will so unbending, but at least this confirmed that he hadn't done it with malice.

A knock at the front door startled her, and she rose and looked out the window. A black Range Rover was parked by the gate. She'd been so absorbed in the letter she hadn't heard it pull up. Craning her neck, she could make out a woman's form standing underneath the overhang by the front door.

Hastily folding the note into the back pocket of her jeans, she rushed down the stairs. She paused for a fraction of a second before opening the front door, then berated herself for being so suspicious. It was Huntersford Leigh in broad daylight, for god's sake. It was more likely to be someone collecting for the church bazaar than her father's killer.

Any doubt was pushed firmly aside as she was greeted with a friendly smile.

"Hi. I'm Ella. I work with Judge." She looked up at the outside of the cottage just above the door. "He said I might find you here."

Grace frowned. Something was off. The woman's expression held a wary regard.

"Hi," she replied, shaking the woman's outstretched hand. Her stomach twisted as the smile dropped and concern took over Ella's expression.

"I'm afraid there's been an accident."

A cold chill swept over Grace.

The shock must have registered on her face because Ella immediately held up a hand. "Don't panic, everything is fine. Judge is just resting up at the hospital waiting for some tests to check they've not missed anything. He asked if I could come and pick you up."

Grace relaxed a fraction, and innate politeness took over at the kindness of a stranger. "You didn't need to do that. He should have called. I could have got someone to drive me over." She peered out the doorway. "The weather's still not too bad."

"I think his phone got lost in the accident. If you come with me, I can take you to him."

"It's fine. Tell me where he is and I'll arrange something. I don't want to be a bother."

Ella inclined her head. "Seriously. He'll give me grief if I don't drive you."

Grace forced a laugh. "That sounds like Dev. I wouldn't want to get you into trouble. I'll just get my coat and bag."

Maybe her dad was right. She should stop hiding behind the lens of a shutter and trust people that only wanted to help her.

Her phone rang as she followed Ella up the path towards the SUV. Devlin appeared on the caller ID. Thank goodness. She'd been so worried.

"So you found your phone?"

"What?" Confusion clouded his tone.

"Ella said you'd lost it in the accident." Grace looked ahead. The friendliness in Ella's face had gone.

"Grace, I don't know what you're talking about. There's been no accident. Where are you?"

"At home. I mean Dad's place." No accident? She tried to work through the permutations. Why had Ella lied?

Then she froze, spotting the damage to the front of the Range Rover at the same time as Ella reached behind her and pulled out a handgun.

"Ditch the phone and get in," Ella told her. "You're driving."

Devlin's voice, cool, controlled, and laced with dread, brought her out of her momentary shock.

"Grace? Ella is Ronnie's wife. Just do what she says. We're on our way."

Pushing aside the cold chill sweeping through his body, threatening to freeze him in panic, Devlin picked up the internal phone and dialled Jamie's extension. He cut across his friend's greeting. "Ella's got Grace."

Jamie cursed under his breath. "I'll see you outside in five."

"Thanks. I'll grab us some gear." He had no idea where Ella was likely to go, but they needed to be prepared for anything. Especially in this weather.

Jamie was as good as his word. As Devlin stepped out of the office doors, he pulled up in front in his Land Cruiser.

Devlin threw the holdall containing the equipment he'd picked up on his way down in the back of the vehicle and climbed into the passenger seat.

Jamie peered at the side mirror as he pulled out onto the main road. "Where do we start?"

"Geoff's place. That's where Grace was." His jaw clenched. "Even though I told her to stay at mine today."

Jamie shot him a sympathetic look. "She'll be okay. She's smart, resourceful, and used to working on her own."

"I hope you're right. Ella's got a gun."

"You sure?"

"She expected Grace to comply. If it had been anything else Grace would have just run."

"Fuck."

Devlin pulled his phone out of his pocket, just in case Grace tried to contact him again, even though his gut said it was wishful thinking. "I should have thought of this yesterday."

"Why?"

Devlin glanced across at him. "You weren't at home yesterday evening?" There was no way he'd have missed the fire if he had been.

"No. Did I miss something?"

"My parents' barn was set on fire."

"Shit. Are they okay?"

"They're fine, but something Jared said about mixing up the house names suddenly made me realise that maybe Geoff wasn't the intended target."

Jamie frowned as he took the road out towards Huntersford. "But your parents are just as unlikely a target as Geoff."

"Yeah, but I'm not."

Jamie's eyes widened. "You think Ella's out for revenge?"

"I can't see who else it would be." It seemed unbelievable, which is why he hadn't considered it. He prayed it wouldn't be another mistake he'd live to regret. "Not that I'd call it revenge. Grief, maybe Anger. Loss."

"Fucking unhinged is what I'd call it."

Yeah. There was that too. He just hoped nothing would happen to Grace. There might still be a lot of uncertainty between them, but he'd been hoping that she might reconsider leaving Huntersford Leigh for good.

Jamie cursed as he pulled out to overtake a line of traffic going slowly in the pouring rain.

"Have you any idea where Ella might go?" Devlin asked.

"Damn. Should have thought of it before. Hold that thought." He hit the contacts on the screen, and there was a short ring, then Geordie's familiar voice answered. "What's up?"

"Did you place the tracker like I asked?"

"Of course."

Devlin shot Jamie a look. In combat situations he wouldn't think twice about it, but unsanctioned use of company property was the fastest way to be shown the door at Agema. The holdall full of gear on the back seat meant he'd have his own apologising to do. Not that it would have stopped him this time.

Jamie shrugged. "Walt knows. I figured if Ella was a suicide risk, we should at least be able to reach her quickly if she called one of us."

Devlin exhaled deeply. Walt. Holder of company secrets. One step down from the board, giving them the plausible deniability they needed to pacify shareholders when things went south, but no less powerful because of it.

Walt was the glue they needed to function in the real world, where good and bad often melded into a murky grey. Ronnie had never worked for Agema, but Walt would understand their need to look after the family of someone who was once their own.

Devlin leant closer to the dash. "Do you know where she was on Monday about seventeen hundred hours?"

"I'll check," Geordie said.

Jamie gave a slight shake of his head. "That never occurred to me."

"Don't beat yourself up. It didn't to me, either."

Geordie came back on the line. "Have the vehicle on the B3212 heading out of Exeter at seventeen ten on Monday."

Devlin cursed under his breath.

"What's her current location?" Jamie asked.

"Heading away from Huntersford Leigh up towards the Okehampton range."

"Good. Stay on it. We should be at Huntersford in about ten minutes."

Devlin hit his thigh with his fist. "The flags were up yesterday."

Geordie's voice came back over the speaker. "Yep. Just checked and the range is live day and night this week. Do you want me to see if I can notify someone?"

Devlin knew it would probably be pointless. High-paced, tactical training didn't get cancelled because someone had wandered onto the range. On the plus side, it was highly likely they'd be spotted before they came across anything too serious. He hoped.

"Yeah. Can you tell Walt too?" He'd be pissed off about the equipment, but there was no point in really getting on his bad side if some army high-up complained to him.

Jamie started to indicate as the turning for Huntersford came up. "Fastest way towards the range is to carry on?"

"No. We don't know for certain Grace is in the car. I want to make sure she didn't get left behind at the cottage, injured. The wind and rain will be much worse up there already, and the risk from exposure is too great."

Despite the inclement weather, they made it to Geoff's place in record time, but a quick look around revealed the situation was as Devlin had feared. Grace had presumably gone to the cottage to sort through more stuff before Ella turned up.

"There's a phone over here," Jamie confirmed.

His heart sank when he saw Grace's phone on the edge of the path leading to the house. He walked round to the rear of the cottage and broke in through the back door. He wanted to be certain the house was empty. There was no sign of Grace's coat or handbag, so he had to presume that until the moment he rang her, she was getting in the car willingly.

They didn't have time to waste.

Jamie was already back in the Cruiser. "Where next?"

"Let's follow the tracker sand hope we don't lose them in this weather."

"Geordie called back. He's heard back from someone at the range and they'll let the wardens know. He warned them Ella might be armed. Apparently, the action is all over this side of the moor. They're taking advantage of the weather to put everyone through some rough training. Poor bastards."

Devlin swallowed hard. Being on the range when it was live at any time was asking for trouble. But in low light levels, in the middle of a storm, it would be suicidal if someone didn't spot them first. He prayed Grace would find some way to escape. But Ella had seen action herself. That was how she and Ronnie had met, and as smart as Grace was, he didn't think she'd be a physical match for Ella.

"Let's go. I'll call Callum and get him to meet us there. If they take off on foot, we'll need all the help we can get, and there'll be no getting a heli up in this weather."

Chapter Twenty

Grace's fingers were white as her grip tightened on the steering wheel. She was driving as fast as she dared. When they'd started off, the roads hadn't been too bad, but higher up on the moor the rain was already pooling at the side of the road.

Grace darted a sideways look at Ella. "Where are we going?"

"You'll see soon enough."

A slither of fear snaked across Grace's shoulders. She hadn't noticed it before, but the woman's eyes were lit a little too brightly. Drugs? Or just adrenalin? Did it make a difference? She had the barrel of a gun trained on Grace either way.

Maybe she could make her see sense. That whatever was wrong surely wasn't worth this. That it was taking things too far, until there was no going back. Just like she and her dad. Her breath hitched. Is that what they'd done?

The car fishtailed as she took a corner too fast, and she struggled to regain control. Even with the windscreen wipers at full pelt she could barely see where she was going. It wouldn't be long before they would be forced to stop.

"Devlin won't be far behind." She hoped.

"I'm planning on it."

That didn't sound good. What did Ella have planned? Grace didn't want to be responsible for him coming to her rescue, only to walk into a trap. Maybe there'd be a way to warn him.

She eased her foot off the accelerator. "If that's the case, maybe we should wait for him now."

Ella's mouth twisted in disdain. "You're so pathetic. All ready to do his bidding. You didn't even hesitate when I said I'd take you to him." She frowned as she noticed the drop in speed and raised the gun that had started to droop in her hand. "Keep driving."

Grace made the pretence of speeding up a little. Maybe if she could slow down enough, it would give Devlin the chance to catch up. "Why don't we stop now and wait for him? Talk this all out."

"Just like Denise. She'd do anything for Judge, and he walked her into a trap. Well, now he's about to get a taste of his own medicine. Find out what it's like to lose someone you love."

The note suddenly made sense. *You killed her.* It had been meant for Devlin, except this woman couldn't have known that Devlin lived over the other side of the village now or that the two Moors Cottages were constantly getting mixed up.

Fear forgotten, anger flowed through her veins. "You killed my father."

"Yeah. I didn't realise until you turned up. I was in the car with Jamie one time when he said he needed to drop something off for Judge's father's surprise party. It never occurred to me it wasn't the right house." Ella slumped further back in her seat, contempt on her face. "Casualty of war, isn't that what they call it?"

"But it wasn't my father's war." He was fighting his own battles and she was only just beginning to realise how hard they'd been for him. "Why?"

"Why?!" Ella sat up straight with an air of disbelief. "Why the fuck do you think? Because he took everything away from me without a single regret."

"But it wasn't like that. If you'd only talk to Devlin, maybe he could help you understand."

"Turn left on the path up here."

Grace briefly looked across to the passenger seat, acutely aware of the gun pointed at her. She didn't want to argue, but if memory served her correctly, turning left would take them up onto the range, and she'd already seen the red flags further back. "But the flags are raised."

Ella laughed off her concern. "We're only going round the edge. It will be fine."

Grace frowned. That wasn't how she remembered it. They'd been torn off a strip by a warden once when they were kids for examining the remains of a piece of ordnance that hadn't been picked up. The flags hadn't even been raised that time.

On the other hand, maybe she'd have a better chance of escape if they came across a military exercise. She already had one live gun trained on her. What was one more?

The rain was coming down even harder, and the path Ella had them on was slick with mud already. The car slipped a little to the left. Grace frantically tried to remember what she'd been taught. Did you drive into a skid? Or was that only on ice, not mud?

The car swerved to the right, the tail spun out, and the car spun slowly three hundred and sixty degrees. As it started to come to a halt, she tried to correct the steering, but with no grip on the road all she succeeded in doing was putting it into a faster spin, and they careered off the side of the road.

"What the fuck are you doing?" Ella screeched, waving the gun in her hand in a way that would have alarmed Grace, had it not been that now the car was gathering speed down the slope. She kept pressing the brake pedal but it was hopeless. She tried to ease the handbrake up, but nothing seemed to slow their descent.

Eventually, the car came to an abrupt halt as it slammed into the side of a rocky outcrop. It started to tilt upwards and Grace screamed as it was about to flip, but at the last moment gravity won and the car slammed back down onto the ground, banging her head on the side of the window.

Miraculously, a headlight was still on, but all Grace could see was moorland. Maybe it would make them easier to find. She closed her eyes, the pain in her head throbbing unbearably. The distant fire of guns made her cringe. But she'd take the chances of a stray bullet or a tank hitting her over being cornered by a mad woman any day.

A groan next to her forced her into action. Glancing around the car, she couldn't see the gun. Using all her might, she forced open the driver's door and fell sideways into the mud.

"The turning should be just up ahead." Devlin twisted his fingers across the screen to enlarge the image. The vehicle tracker hadn't moved for the last thirty minutes.

He refused to let his mind go over possible scenarios. The signal up here was patchy at best. He'd be no help to Grace if he let his worst fears takeover.

"Yeah. I can just make out some tracks in the mud." Jamie peered through the windscreen. "I'm hoping the second set of tyres is Callum."

"I messaged him the location twenty minutes ago. Can't see anyone else being out in this."

"There's a set of muddy tyre tracks beyond the turning, like they came out of here." Jamie's voice held a hint of hesitation.

Devlin understood Jamie was giving him a choice. At work, Jamie was the lead operator, no doubt about it, but going after Grace was personal.

"Make the turn. The car might hold some clue to their destination even if it's empty."

The path was hard going even in the four by four, but eventually they saw the lights of Callum's search and rescue vehicle. He and another guy were busy unloading gear. There was no sign of another car and Devlin's heart sank.

Callum approached as Jamie brought the car to a halt. Devlin jumped out and started firing questions at Callum, but his friend just held up a hand to stop him.

"There's an SUV gone off the road and down the slope." He pointed further down the path. "It's empty."

Devlin stepped forward and looked down the hill. A vehicle was lying partially on its side against a rock. He let out a sigh. There was still a chance that this would turn out okay. At least his worst fear—that Ella would have already shot Grace before turning the gun on herself—had been allayed.

"Any sign of them?"

"Yeah. There are footprints leading away. I'm guessing from the way the rain is starting to mask the first pair, someone has had a few minutes' head start."

Devlin's stomach churned. It had to be Grace in front. If it was the other way around, Grace would have stayed put. "We need to catch up with them before Ella does something stupid."

Callum looked down at the Range Rover. "Think she's already past that. Come on, John's got some wet-weather gear in the back of the Land Rover."

Jamie had already snagged the holdall from the back of his car and was stuffing extra equipment from it into the rucksack John had given him.

He looked up as they approached. "Thanks, Callum. We owe you mate."

"No problem. Let's hope we find them in time."

The wind whipped around them, and Devlin cursed the minutes it took to prepare, but he knew Callum was right. In this storm, they'd pretty soon become casualties themselves if they didn't have the right clothing.

When they reached Ella's vehicle he punched the bonnet with the side of his fist in frustration. "Why didn't she head towards the road?"

"A lot of people lose their sense of direction, especially if she's sustained a head injury. And look at it—we can barely see in front of our noses."

Callum's words made sense but did little to ease Devlin's frustration. "She'd have followed the path, presuming it would take her somewhere. The prints look fresh."

At least the four of them should be able to catch up quickly. The two women were fit, but they had the advantage of a longer stride. He surged on ahead, following the path, leaving the others to follow him.

While he fixed his focus on what tracks he could see in the mud, the others tried to look around them, as much as visibility would allow.

The sudden change in the patterns made Devlin pull up short. He lifted his head and the rain hitting him sideways blurred his vision. He blinked to clear it and scanned the immediate area. "There's a third set joining them. Look." He pointed to the new set of prints. What the hell?

"Soldier?" Callum suggested.

"Not unless he's wearing heels," Jamie commented, staring down at the footprints. "And they're fresher. The rain hasn't messed with these yet. Once we're over the next rise, we should be able to see them."

They set off again as fast as they could. After several minutes, a dark form spread out on the ground started to materialise in the driving rain. As they drew closer, Devlin could see a person lying face down in the mud. He ran forward, adrenalin providing the extra push his muscles needed to overcome the cold that was seeping in.

Despite Callum and John turning up with search and rescue gear, he and Jamie were still not adequately dressed for the long trek through a heavy storm. Though not as unprepared as the person in front of them.

His heart hammered in his chest as he approached the still form. He didn't recognise the thin coat and woollen hat. Leaning down, he turned the body over.

Devlin didn't know whether to be relieved that it wasn't Grace or despair that they still hadn't found her. "What are the chances of finding a body we weren't looking for?"

"Higher than you'd think," Callum said with a grim smile as he bent down. "There's always more than one person that pays no heed to the weather warnings. She's got a pulse. Not great, but she's alive."

But was Grace? Devlin turned to Jamie. "Which way now?"

"I think they should be just up ahead. The tracks pick up again just over there." He pointed off to the right of a craggy outcrop.

The wind lulled for a moment, and distant gunfire could be heard, an eerie reminder of exactly where they were. He hoped it was further away than it sounded. Although with luck someone would have already noticed their presence on the range, and they'd soon have company.

He looked back at Callum, who was already going over the body checking for breakages.

Callum lifted his chin. "You go on, mate. John and I can handle this. She'll weigh hardly anything, and we've got everything we need in John's pack. It won't be long till we can get back to the cars and assess her there."

He reached for the backpack he'd shrugged off moments before and handed it to Devlin. "Here, take my pack. Everything's in there. First aid, heat blanket, even a makeshift stretcher, if you need it."

Devlin didn't waste time arguing. He knew his friend was more than capable of handling the situation. Mumbling his thanks, he grabbed the pack and strode off to follow Jamie, more than aware that although the woman had only delayed them a minute or two, it was time Grace might not have to spare.

They continued forward, slogging through driving rain and wind strong enough to take his breath away. But with each step, the tracks were becoming more and more patchy.

"What do you want to do if we don't catch sight of them soon?"

Devlin steeled himself against the ache in his heart. Jamie had voiced the question he'd already asked himself. Continue until they did, was what he wanted to answer, but he knew as well as anyone that would be suicide in these conditions. It was easy enough to get turned around on the moor at night and lose the way, but at least you could see some of the landmarks. The rain, wind and low cloud was seriously hindering visibility. They'd need to regroup and come up with a different plan.

Devlin turned to Jamie. His friend's face was full of sympathy.

"Just a bit further, mate. Up to the next ridge. You remember that abandoned house we used to hang out at sometimes?"

Jamie nodded.

"Well, maybe Grace does too."

They continued on.

"Wish we still had that tracker," Devlin said. "You didn't think to put it on her mobile?"

"Too obvious," replied Jamie. "Besides, you know you'd never get a signal up here. They can't be much further ahead."

His friend steamed past him with a sudden burst of energy now the top of the ridge was near.

By the time he reached the top, Devlin had almost caught him up again.

"Shit."

"What is it?" Devlin scrambled over the rocky terrain. His heart hammered in his chest as much from Jamie's tone as from the exertion.

As he reached the summit of a small peak, the rain eased and his heart caught at the scene laid out before them.

Two figures in the distance, one chasing the other, heading towards a cottage.

CHAPTER TWENTY-ONE

Blood pounded in Grace's ears. She'd never run so hard in her life. There was no escaping Ella, but if she could find somewhere to hide in the abandoned cottage, she might be able to buy herself some time and give Devlin a chance to find them.

Her hopes had risen when she first saw the cottage, remembering it from years ago. But in the few seconds she'd paused to get her bearings in the rain, Ella had closed the gap between them.

If she was to stand a chance, she needed to speed up. But while her trainers had been fine for the short walk across the village this morning, they were no match for the wet and the cold out on the moor.

She'd lost the feeling in her feet a while ago, and her hands were frozen too. She'd tried keeping them in her pockets, but that made it even harder to run. The only consolation was that it looked like Ella was having a hard time, too.

She reached the cottage and let out a sigh of relief when the door swung open easily. But her heart sank when she realised there was nothing in the room to prop the door shut. Although with a couple of windows missing glass, there was probably little point.

She'd be better searching for somewhere to hide if she wanted to avoid being caught by Ella straightaway. Then hopefully she'd still be in a position to shout out and warn Devlin about the gun. If he arrived.

When he arrives, she corrected herself. She needed to believe he would find them.

She walked quickly into the next room. A large inglenook fireplace dominated the end wall. She ran over and looked up. If she had to, she might be able to climb up and brace her feet to hide inside. But she wouldn't be able to stay there long.

She placed her foot on the first step of the stairs and realised there'd be no hiding from Ella. Or at least not for very long. Her wet footprints hadn't shown up on the cottage's stone floor, because it was already wet. But the stairs were wood.

It wasn't just her footprints that would give her away. The rain still dripping off her clothes would soak into the wood too. There was nothing she could do now but to try to avoid Ella for as long as possible.

She ran up the staircase, dismayed to see how small and bare the upstairs was. From the window, she could see Ella was almost at the cottage. It wouldn't be long before she caught up.

But then more movement outside caught her attention, further back along the way she and Ella had approached the cottage. She peered harder into the gloom and saw it again. She stared transfixed, desperate for the rain to slow a little so she could see more clearly.

Suddenly a gust of wind blew the rain sideways, and she caught a glimpse of two figures making their way towards the cottage. She just had to hold on a bit longer, knowing that help was on its way.

She whipped her head around the open space and hurried over to the furthest, darkest corner and crouched down. She pulled her knees up hard against herself, wrapped her arms around them, and bent her head to make herself as small as possible. It wasn't much, but it might give her a few more precious seconds.

"Fuck me, it's as cold as a witch's tit." Ella's words resounded around the empty building from downstairs, along with the sound of her stomping her feet.

Grace tucked her head even tighter into her knees.

"You in here, Grace?"

She pressed her lips inwards, scared she'd make a sound and give herself away.

"Yes. I know you're here. It's too bloody cold to stay out there any longer."

Ella's voice drifted back and forth. She must be looking around downstairs, just as Grace had done.

"Not coming out to play?"

The voice boomed through the fireplace just behind her, almost startling her into crying out. She'd been right not to try to hide in the chimney.

"Well, that's fine. I can wait."

Fainter again. Ella had stepped away from the hearth downstairs. But now the silence frightened Grace more. Surely she'd seen the footprints on the stairs by now.

"Okay, girly. We've got company. Now where are you?"

The stairs creaked. It wouldn't be long until Ella found her. If her damp footprints didn't give her away, she was certain her thundering heartbeat would.

"Grace, there's nowhere to hide in here." Another tread squeaked as Ella came slowly up the stairs.

She could cower here in the corner or stand up and take her chances. Damn. She should have hidden behind the door. Was it too late to make her way across the room now?

"Judge is on his way to rescue you and we're going to put on a little show for him. You want to cooperate, don't you, Grace?"

She risked edging across the room, while Ella was talking, praying the floorboards didn't cave. As she drew closer, she could spy Ella through the crack in the jamb, nearing the top of the stairs, gun at the ready.

"I can see you're behind the door, Grace, so you might as well come out."

Was she bluffing, or could she really see her?

Ella kicked the door with her foot, and Grace slammed it back, hoping to at least unbalance the other woman, but all she succeeded in doing was making her more angry.

"Now that wasn't nice, was it Grace?"

This time the door opened with force and Grace stepped further along the wall as Ella burst in, her gun raised, ready to fire.

When they were in the car, Grace had felt certain that Ella wouldn't shoot her, but now she was truly afraid. So scared, she was almost calm. What was the worst that could happen now?

As she moved again, Ella trained the gun on her. "Stand still."

Grace stopped where she was. The only thing she could do was hope she could keep Ella talking long enough for whoever it was out there to arrive.

"Would Ronnie really want you to be doing this?"

Ella's face contorted even more. Her hand shook slightly, but she kept the gun aimed at Grace. "Don't call her that. Her name's not Ronnie. It's Denise."

"I'm sorry. I didn't know."

"No. I don't suppose Judge ever saw her as I did. They all hide behind their silly little nicknames. Her surname was Barker, so naturally, they called her Ronnie. Thought it was so clever."

An image of the iconic comedian flashed into Grace's mind. A bubble of hysterical laughter caught in her throat as the very real possibility that her last thought on earth might be the fork handle sketch sank in.

She cleared her throat. "I think Devlin had the utmost respect for Denise and the work she did."

Ella huffed dismissively and held up her gun hand a little straighter. "It's Denise's gun. A little souvenir from her first deployment in Iraq that she kept hidden away. Quite poetic, don't you think?"

Grace's legs and arms were starting to shake. She couldn't tell if it was fear or the cold. Either way, it made it almost impossible to answer Ella. Not that she seemed to notice.

"Now you and I are going to take a walk down the stairs nice and slowly and wait for your boyfriend to show up."

Grace didn't bother to correct her misconception. She couldn't decide if it would anger or appease the other woman. Instead she put all her focus into getting down the stairs. She gripped the railing as tight as she could, worried that at any moment her legs would give way.

"Stop right there and turn towards the door."

She paused by the inglenook fireplace and did as Ella said. Using her height advantage, Ella came up behind her and placed her arm around Grace's throat in a headlock.

The outside door flew open, and Jamie burst through the doorway, immediately stepping to the other side.

Ella pulled Grace a little closer and pressed the steel barrel against Grace's temple, her hand shaking just a fraction as she did so.

"Where the hell is Judge?"

"He was busy." Jamie's voice floated out of the broken window Devlin was crouched down behind.

He'd vetoed Devlin going in first. Ella was too unstable. The situation might rapidly get out of control if they gave her what she wanted—to harm Grace and make Devlin suffer.

He risked peeking over the top of the window ledge, knowing Ella would be distracted for a few seconds. As they'd both assumed, she was using Grace as a shield.

He'd seen some horrors in his time, but he'd always held it together. The training to remain cool and calm always kicked in, no matter what the situation.

But the sight of Grace pale and frightened, having the breath squeezed out of her as Ella tightened her grip, released a primitive fury inside of him.

He ducked down as Ella started to look around her, suddenly realising her position wasn't as strong as she'd thought.

He closed his eyes and took a second to collect himself. They had the advantage, so long as he remained focused and acted quickly.

"Where is he? I know you didn't come alone."

He could hear her scuffling on the floor. It would be difficult for her to maintain her hold on Grace and watch the windows on either side of her.

"Come out, you cowardly bastard."

He pulled the trigger on the smoke bomb and gave a low whistle to warn Jamie as he lobbed it through the window.

Taking advantage of Ella's momentary distraction by the dense cloud of smoke, he leapt up from his position and bounded through the opening. His arms clasped around Grace, pulling her from Ella's grasp, and he rolled with her until she was behind him, out of the line of fire.

A scream of rage poured out of Ella as she raised her gun towards him. Then a sudden movement to her side as Jamie charged across the room caught her off guard. She'd been so focused on Grace and Devlin, she'd forgotten about him.

He knocked her over, and the gun flew out of her hand. She crawled towards it, while Jamie tried to catch her ankle. Devlin pounced on it at the same time as her fingers clasped around the trigger. The shot went wide, but it ricocheted off the stone walls and a searing pain shot up Devlin's thigh.

Fuck.

Ella rolled over with the gun, the heels of her trainers scrabbling over the stone floor as she propped herself up against the fireplace. She moved the gun between Devlin and Jamie. "Stop. Don't come any closer."

"Just put the gun down, Ella." Jamie spoke slowly and clearly, even though he was breathing hard from the exertion. "It doesn't have to be like this."

He took a step towards her. She placed a second hand on the gun to firm her grip. "Stop."

Devlin tried to move closer from his position, but with his leg shot he didn't have his usual stealth and he gave himself away. Ella swung the barrel towards him. "You too."

Behind him, Grace gasped. He hoped Ella didn't hear it. The last thing he wanted was Ella to be training her gun on Grace again.

"What are you hoping to achieve, Ella?" Jamie asked.

"Justice. Justice for Denise."

"You think killing Devlin is going to do that?"

Devlin knew what Jamie was doing. By calling him Devlin, he was trying to humanise him to Ella. But he didn't deserve it. He was responsible for Ronnie's death, as much as he was responsible for Geoff's and for putting Grace's life in danger. He was never going to forgive himself, so why expect others to?

"Maybe not, but it will make me feel better."

She tightened her grip on the butt of the gun and pulled the trigger, shooting Devlin in the chest.

Grace screamed as Devlin fell backwards from the momentum of the bullet. In his peripheral vision, he saw Jamie tackle Ella again. Another shot was fired, and then there was no more movement, only silence.

A second later, Jamie got to his feet and walked over, holding out his hand. "You okay?"

Devlin took it and hauled himself up on his good leg. "I'll survive. Hurts like fuck, though."

Grace frowned at Devlin, her face a mixture of puzzlement and shock.

"Bullet-proof vests," Jamie explained. "We're mad, but not stupid."

Before he could say any more, a half a dozen soldiers stormed the building.

Chapter Twenty-Two

The unmistakable sounds and smell of a hospital were the first thing that filtered through Grace's consciousness as she woke. Her head pounded and she had a raging thirst, but at least she finally felt warm.

She opened her eyes just enough to get her bearings. Across the dimly lit room she could make out Jess' form, sat in a chair beside the window. She closed her eyes again and dozed, but something was nagging at the back of her mind.

Suddenly, it all came back. She sucked in a breath and sat bolt upright, startling Jess out of her chair.

"Devlin." The last thing she remembered was being wrapped in a heat blanket and loaded into an army truck.

Pushing the bedclothes away, she tried to stand. Her legs weren't as steady as she expected. Jess took a hold of her arm and forced her back down onto the bed.

"He's okay."

"But I need to see him. Is he here? What happened?" Grace tried to get up again, but Jess placed a hand on her shoulder and pressed her back down into the pillow.

"Relax. You're not going anywhere until the doctor says so." She lifted the bedcovers back over Grace. "Besides, you've only just stopped shivering with the hypothermia, the last thing you need to be doing is running around half naked in a hospital gown in the middle of the night."

Tears pricked the back of Grace's eyes. "But I need to see him, Jess."

A stern expression crossed her friend's face. "You're supposed to stay here and keep warm. He's fine, I promise you. He's in surgery, anyway."

"Surgery! You said he's fine. That's not fine."

Her hand went for the covers again, but Jess was still holding them firmly down.

"I swear he's okay. It's just to remove the bullet. There is nothing you can do at the moment. You wouldn't be able to see him. Now go back to sleep and next time you wake up, maybe they'll let you visit."

She clasped Jess' hand. "You promise me he's all right."

"Yeah, he's fine. Nothing's going to slow that knucklehead down."

Jess smiled, her eyes full of sympathy, and Grace took comfort that her friend wouldn't have looked so calm if Devlin was in any real danger. Not like he'd been in the house on the moor.

Realisation of the extent of his injury suddenly dawned on her. "Oh." She sank back onto the pillow, defeated.

Jess misunderstood her reaction. "I promise you he's going to be fine."

"No, it's not that. Don't you see? With this injury he's never going to be able to get back in the field. He's ruined his chance by rescuing me, and if I'd done what he told me to do and stayed away from the house, he never would have needed to."

Jess sat on the side of the bed and gave her a hug. "Shush, sweetie. You're getting yourself all upset. I'm sure Devlin doesn't think of it that way at all." She released Grace and sat back, her face creased in agitation. "And if he does, then he's a jerk, and we shall both hate him forever."

A warmth spread through her chest at her friend's staunch defence of her idiocy. Because this really was all her fault.

"I found a note from my dad. Just before Ella knocked on the door. I think that's why I was too slow to react initially."

Jess squeezed Grace's hand and winced apologetically. "I know. I moved your clothes, and it fell out of the back pocket of your jeans."

"Did you read it?"

Jess shrugged. "You know me, I couldn't resist it."

Any other time, she'd have probably been extremely irritated with Jess, but right now she didn't have the energy. Besides, Jess was right—she hadn't changed a bit since they were little, and there was something comforting in that. "We'll make a Weird Sister out of you yet."

Jess gasped in mock horror. "Grace Vaughan, you take that back."

Grace gave her a half-hearted smile. "I still don't understand it, though. How could he have possibly thought that making me stay here a year was going to make a difference?"

"Yeah. You only needed a couple of weeks."

Grace frowned. Sometimes Jess spoke in riddles.

"We all love you, you daft girl. We never stopped. You just weren't around for us to show our appreciation. Don't think now you're back you can go running off again. I'm pretty sure Devlin will have something to say about that."

Grace's heart clenched. She was certain he would too, but she didn't think it would be very complimentary after all the trouble she'd caused.

Devlin took a sip of water and reclined against the pillow with a sigh. He was irritable and restless. The last thing he wanted was to be stuck in hospital, but he'd already been told he wouldn't be discharged for at least a few days.

He was desperate to see Grace. To check for himself that she was okay. The only thing that had calmed him was learning that Jamie had thought to phone Jess. Grace needed a friendly face right now. He'd hated to think of her alone after the ordeal with Ella.

The door to the room opened and Jamie strode in, predictably followed by a nurse asking if he needed anything. She barely looked at Devlin besides giving his chart a cursory glance.

Devlin coughed.

"What?" Jamie asked as the nurse left. "Can't help it if I'm a babe magnet."

"Yeah. You keep telling yourself that. Once of these days it's gonna get you into trouble."

Jamie slumped down in the chair opposite and Devlin frowned.

"How come you're not tied up with the police?"

"Commanding Officer told me to get in the ambulance with Grace, that I was suffering from hypothermia and to leave the rest with him. I wasn't going to argue. Civilian shooting, in the middle of live training, probably on Duchy land too, with my luck. It'll be a mess."

Devlin nodded his response. Jamie was right. Either they would all claim it was their right to investigate, or none of them would want to touch it.

Jamie grimaced. "I think you and I are going to get a bollocking from Walt though."

Devlin had no doubt about that. Between the pair of them, they'd broken nearly every rule in the company handbook. "What happened in the end?"

"We went down. The gun went off. Her finger was on the trigger, but did she mean for it to hit me or her..." Jamie frowned and gave a slight shake of his head. "I don't know. Guess we never will."

Devlin sighed. It was all so pointless. The death. The destruction. The lives ruined. He glanced down at his leg. No going back in the field for him now. He knew it had a been a long shot anyway, even if he hadn't been prepared to admit it.

Jamie had joked earlier about him being as good as new. But this, on top of the other injury, was a deal-breaker. He didn't need a doctor to tell him. He'd seen it before.

Thinking about doctors reminded him of something. "Hey. What happened about that other body? I've started to think I dreamt it."

"It's real. And currently sleeping soundly in Callum's bed."

Devlin raised his brow.

"He says she refused to go to hospital and since there was nothing wrong with her aside from mild hypothermia, he didn't see the point in pushing the issue. Especially since the ambulance crews were already overstretched with the severe weather."

"So he took her home with him?"

Jamie smirked. "I think she's actually in the surgery, but my version sounds more interesting."

Devlin rolled his eyes. With the exception of work, getting Jamie to take anything seriously was a challenge. "I still find it bizarre that we were looking for Grace and found someone else instead."

"According to Cal, they had a similar incident a couple of years ago. They were looking for a walker who'd gone missing and came across a cyclist that had fallen off his bike and concussed his head."

"So what was she doing up there?"

"He doesn't know."

"But..."

"Stop worrying. He's a grown man. It's not like either of us thinks the girl is in danger from him. I'll drop by later."

A noise outside the room made them both turn their heads towards the door. Jess was hovering in the hallway, with Grace at her side. A warmth spread through his chest at the sight of her. He started to get up, but then silently cursed as he remembered he was trapped in the bed for the time being, with bandages wrapped around his thigh.

Jess' gaze darted between him and Jamie. "Hi Devlin, glad to see you're okay. If you're up for a visit, I can leave Grace here with you for a few minutes, while Jamie and I grab a coffee?"

Not normally one to take the hint so easily, Jamie quickly vacated his chair and moved it closer to the bed, giving Devlin a wink as Jess settled Grace into it.

Grace muttered her thanks to Jess as she and Jamie left the room. Then she stared down at her hands in her lap.

"Hi." He'd been waiting all this time to see her and now suddenly he didn't know what to say. "Are you okay?"

She looked up. The caution he saw in her eyes had him confused. Not that he could blame her. It was his fault her father died.

"I'm fine. Jess is just fussing. The nurse said I'll be discharged in a few hours. How are you?"

"Okay. The doctor reckons I should be out in a couple of days."

She fidgeted with the cuffs of the blue hospital nightgown sticking out from beneath a robe. "I'm sorry your friend's wife died."

Devlin was floored. "That's a very generous thing to say considering she chased you halfway across the moor." He wasn't even going to think about seeing Grace with a gun barrel to her head. That image was going to give him nightmares for a long time.

"I can't help but feel sorry for her. She lost everything. Or everything that mattered. Grief does strange things to people."

It was the last thing he expected her to say. But at the same time, it made sense. Ella wasn't to blame for her mental state. If he hadn't had fucked up in Iraq, none of this would have happened.

They sat in silence for a few minutes. He was never any good at small talk. He left that for Jamie. But right now the silence was stretching out a bit too long.

He stared down at his legs. "Guess I'll be needing that spare room again."

Her brow creased. "I'll move my stuff out."

"What? No. Grace, you misunderstood. There's no need for you to leave. I just meant it'll be easier than managing the stairs for a bit."

She shrugged, and Devlin cursed his runaway mouth. What was it about Grace that always made him say the wrong thing?

"I should move back into Dad's place, anyway. I'll be safe there now and it will comply with the will."

"Fuck the will, Grace."

She startled at his vehement tone. Then a ghost of a smile crossed her lips. "But you're the one always telling me I should do what it says."

"Well, maybe I'm wrong. You should do what you want. Who knows what he meant when he drafted the will."

He let out a sigh at her startled expression. "Sorry. I know he was your dad, but seriously, it was a fucked-up thing to do. And I'm an arsehole for not realising it sooner."

Not to mention if it hadn't been for him, there might have been time for Geoff to come to his senses, and Grace would never have known that her father had planned to include conditions in his will. A dullness sat heavy on his chest. He could blame it on the bruising from the bulletproof vest, but he knew it was the weight of regret. There was no way Grace was going to want to have anything to do with him now.

She gave him a shaky smile. "The funny thing is, he left me a letter. I found it yesterday morning. All he wanted was for me to be happy."

He opened his mouth to ask her what else it said just as his folks walked into the room. He clenched his fists in frustration as Grace immediately stood up, hugged his mum, and hastily made her exit like she couldn't wait to get away from him. Although given the circumstances, it was understandable.

As the door closed behind her, Devlin cursed loudly. Strangely for once, his mother smiled instead of telling him off.

Chapter Twenty-Three

Devlin exhaled loudly. It had been nearly a week since he'd seen Grace at the hospital and he was itching to continue their conversation. His breath froze in the cold air in front of his face. He lifted the black iron knocker and let it rap back on its post.

He could hear the radio on the other side of the door, so he was fairly certain she was home. Whether or not she'd talk to him was a different matter.

As she opened the door, his throat closed up. It didn't matter that her hair was scraped back, and she had dust and dirt all over her clothes and a bead of sweat running down her temple. She looked beautiful to him.

He stood there silently for a moment before his voice came back to him. "I thought I'd stop by and say hello."

"Hi." She gave a self-depreciating smile. "Sorry about the state of me. I wasn't expecting company."

"You look fine." *Amazing, to a man who's been desperate to see you.*

She peered around him. "Your mum dropped you off?"

He raised his eyebrows. "Is she still there?" He'd not heard the car pull away, so he presumed she still was.

"Yep."

Amusement lit Grace's eyes, and a faint glimmer of hope that he had a chance caused his stomach to flip.

He grimaced. "Sorry."

She leant against the jamb and placed a hand on her hip. "Maybe she's waiting to see if you need a lift back home."

"I told her not to stay."

"Driving you mad?"

He gazed skywards. "You've no idea. I thought last time was bad enough, but then she was just taking me back and forth to the hospital. Getting her to drop me off at a girl's house makes me feel fifteen all over again."

Grace's smile lit up her face. "I don't believe she ever did that for you. You'd have ridden your bike."

He huffed out a breath. "You know what I mean."

"Which girl?"

He moved a little closer. "Why, jealous?"

"Nope."

She'd hesitated just a fraction, but Devlin wasn't going to call her out for telling a lie. He was an idiot when it came to love, but not that much of one.

She waved to his mum and then turned her attention back to him. "You'd better come in, otherwise I think she'll stay there all day." She stepped to one side to let him through, gave a final wave to his mum, and closed the door. "Go through to the living room. The fire's lit. It will be warmer in there."

He looked around the living room, which seemed emptier than before. Clearing clutter or getting ready to leave? He still wasn't sure. It was one of the reasons he'd got his mum to bring him over. He wouldn't be able to drive for a least another week, and there was no way he was asking Jamie.

"Take a seat. Do you need a stool for your leg?"

He sat down in the armchair closest to the fire. "No, it's okay. I'll rest it later. You've been busy."

Grace took the couch and tucked her feet up under herself. "After finding the letter, it was easier somehow. A lot of stuff I've just boxed up and put upstairs. I'm hoping to persuade Jamie to help me put it into the loft. I've been up there this morning trying to sort things, which is why I look a state."

"You look beautiful."

Her cheeks grew pink and she gave a self-deprecating laugh. "That's very sweet of you to say so, but I saw myself in the hall mirror before I answered the door. I know what I look like."

"And you still answered the door?" he teased, knowing he was living dangerously if he hope she'd let him back into her life.

She threw a cushion across the room at him. He caught it and placed it behind his back as if she'd done him a favour. "Thanks."

She sat back on the sofa and crossed her arms, a frown on her face. Maybe he still hadn't learnt his lesson.

"Jared came to see me."

A burning sensation hit Devlin's gut. He'd expected Jared would be in contact, but that still didn't stop the twinge of concern from taking over. "Yeah? What did he say?"

"He said the Crown Prosecution Service wasn't going to pursue Ella's death."

So there was the answer. Jamie was right. No one wanted to touch it.

"He said they couldn't prove that she was involved in Dad's death, but that it was highly likely, given the circumstances. As far as they're concerned, the investigation is over, bar the paperwork. It was just two tragic accidents."

Devlin leant forward. "How do you feel?"

"I don't think it's really sunk in. Every time I try to make sense of it all, I get more confused." She turned towards the fire and fell silent, staring at the flames.

"This room looks good. Still cosy, but not so untidy." Devlin forced a cheer he didn't quite feel into his tone.

"I figured if I got the house clear, I could do tea and sandwiches back here after the funeral next week."

"What, and welcome Mrs Cole and the other Weird Sisters into your home?"

She laughed at his tone of mock horror, and he was pleased to see her smile again.

"Well, they're all part of the village."

He caught her eye, and his heart swelled. Maybe there was some hope she'd forgive him, too. "That must have been some letter your dad wrote."

A hint of sadness crossed her face and he cursed himself for not keeping his mouth shut.

She stood and walked over to the writing desk. He knew she'd be thinking about the last letter that desk had held. Opening it just enough to reach in, she grabbed the letter. "Here. Read it."

"I didn't mean..."

"I know. I want you to."

Grace handed Dev the letter and sat back on the couch while he read it.

Her dad said all he wanted was for her to be happy, but she'd never been sadder than this moment right now.

She was sure Devlin had just come over out of a sense of duty. He'd promised her father he'd look after her, and he'd more than done that when he saved her out on the moor.

She believed him when he said she should do what she wanted. And the fucking, crazy, stupid thing of it all was that what she wanted was to stay here with him.

But she'd cost him the job he loved.

She swallowed hard. Her chest tightened and tears threatened. She had to stop thinking about this now, otherwise she'd be a mess and she wanted to hold it together until he had gone.

He glanced up as she wiped a finger underneath her eyes.

"Grace?"

She waved a hand in front of her face and gave him a wan smile. "Just ignore me. I'm being sentimental."

He stood stiffly—another reminder—as if she needed it of his injury, and came to sit beside her on the couch. She bit her lip as he tucked a finger under her chin, lifting it gently.

"He wouldn't want you to cry."

He spoke softly, and with such empathy, it was nearly her undoing.

"He was right, you know."

She blinked through her tears, wondering what he meant and trying not to think how much she'd miss that steely gaze of his.

"There's at least one person in Huntersford Leigh that loves you."

She sighed. "Yeah. I know. Jess already told me she does."

His lips quirked in a faint smile. "Okay then, two."

Her breath hitched at his words. Did she really have a chance? She swallowed hard, trying to clear her throat of the emotion that was clogging it. "But I've ruined your life."

He frowned. "I meant what I said earlier. You're beautiful inside and out. I'm hoping that generous heart of yours can find a way to forgive me, too."

Her head shot up, breaking away from his touch. "What on earth do you mean?"

He leant back against the sofa and ran a hand through his hair. "Your dad died because of me."

"Don't be ridiculous, Devlin. I've never thought that."

"No. Because you are too nice."

She shook her head. "No. If I had stayed at your place as you asked, Ella would never have found me here."

"But maybe she'd have caught up with you somewhere else, before we realised it was her."

She clasped his hand. "But she never would have had the chance to shoot you if I hadn't had been so determined to prove to you, my dad and the rest of this whole damned village that I didn't need you. When in truth I was running scared."

He leant over and kissed her. "Not as scared as I was when I saw the gun pointed at your head."

"I'm serious, Devlin. You asked how I can forgive you, but you're not going to be able to go back out in the field, are you?"

"No. But Grace, the truth is, I probably never was. I just didn't want to face it. I thought that if I could work in the field, I could somehow avenge Ronnie's death. But Ella proved that focusing all your energy on retribution builds into an unforgiving rage. The only thing it destroys is the good things left in life. Not the bitterness of the past. For the first time, I accept that. I still believe I made a mistake, one that will haunt me the rest of my life, but it's no longer controlling who I am."

He placed his warm hand on her chest. "And it's your big heart that made me realise it."

"But Devlin, you've lost so much that you've worked for." The tears that she'd tried so hard to hold back flowed like the ford in the village after a storm. He pulled her to him and stroked the back of her head as she sobbed into his shoulder, and it felt so good, she was never going to let go.

"Hey. Shush. No ugly crying, you're not that beautiful," he whispered against her temple.

She laughed and hiccuped at the same time, punching him on the arm for being so mean, even if he was only joking.

He pushed her back a little and ran his hand up the side of her face, brushing back her hair. "There's that smile I love."

A tiny spark of joy cracked through her heart. "You were right when you told me I should have come back sooner."

He shook his head and opened his mouth to argue. She placed her fingers over his mouth to stop him and gave him a tremulous smile when he kissed them.

"I set a hard line for Dad to cross, deep down knowing he'd never be able to. Except I used it as a measure of how much he loved me, not how distraught he was to lose my mother."

Devlin wiped a tear from her cheek. "You shouldn't be so hard on yourself."

"When you went down after Ella fired the gun, I was convinced I'd lost you forever. And I hadn't even told you how I felt. I'd left it too long to tell you I was seriously thinking about staying. That I hoped we could try some sort of long-distance relationship given our respective careers. And that I was falling hopelessly in love with you. I wanted—"

His face broke into a broad smile and he moved closer, slanting his lips over hers, silencing her mid-sentence. He kissed her like he had that first time, slow and sweet, building up to a crescendo where her tongue tangled with his as he stole her breath away.

She placed her hand on his leg to steady herself, and Devlin cursed. Mortified, she sat back. "Oh, god. I'm so sorry. Does it hurt bad? Do you want me to get you something? Jesus Christ, Dev. You have to believe me I'd do anything to take back this mess I've created."

He interrupted her with a kiss again. "Stop worrying. It's fine. I'll survive. And don't tell Jamie, but I might be getting a promotion that puts me in the centre of the action, even if it's still tied to a desk."

He curled a hand around her cheek and pulled her closer. "Besides, there's this girl I've met, and the way she smiles at me, I'm hoping she might stay around."

Leaning back on the sofa, careful to move his injured leg out of the way, he opened his arms and Grace fell into them.

Epilogue

Devlin and Jamie each grabbed a sandwich from the plate his mother was carrying as she went past them from the kitchen.

"If you boys keep doing that every time I go by, there won't be enough to go around." Anna's twinkling eyes belied her scolding tone.

They smirked at each other as she walked off into Grace's living room. His mum, Callum's and Jaime's had insisted on doing the catering as soon as they realised Grace was going to hold the wake after the funeral at home. He, his dad and Jamie, did their part by going to the supermarket over in Okehampton for wine, beer and whisky once it became clear that tea and sandwiches were going to be the only offering.

Though dusk wasn't far off now, it had been the perfect winter's day for saying goodbye. As they'd walked out of the crematorium chapel to the haunting melody of Debussy's Reverie, the sky had been a deep blue, the air crisp, and the warmth of the sun gave false hope that spring was on its way.

Devlin nodded towards the two mums still bustling in the kitchen making more tea and coffee for those that wanted it. "Do you think we'll be like that in thirty years?"

"I wouldn't be wasting my time making tea." Jamie muttered under his breath.

"No. I mean rally around each other. It wasn't until the fire last week that I realised how much they all do for each other. People say blood is thicker than water. But I'm thinking true friendship is worth more."

Jamie clicked his bottle of beer on Devlin's. "I'll drink to that."

It struck him today, as he and Jess stood on either side of Grace in the chapel, her hands holding theirs in a vice like grip, how little had changed from the days of forming a snake under Mrs Hargreaves' supervision on school days out. Except that at the same time, death and destruction in all their lives had changed everything.

"Any idea yet where Geoff was going?" Jamie asked.

"None. Jared said they'd followed up phone records, emails, etc. But nothing stood out." He shrugged. "I guess we'll never know. Maybe if he'd been on another road, it would have been a different story."

"Someone might have found him sooner, or the tree wouldn't have been there."

Devlin hummed his agreement. "I know Grace thinks about that often. Same 'what ifs' as I do about Iraq."

"You know you can't think like that. Supposing Geoff had collided with another car, or you called a halt to the operation after the whole team went in. There's always a worse outcome to wishful 'what-ifs'."

"All actions have consequences." He drained the last of his beer and set the bottle down on the hallway table.

Jamie was right, change was inevitable in life. One just had to adapt. He turned to look at Grace as she came through the living room doorway. But life was infinitely better now that Grace was right there next to him.

She handed him her empty wineglass, sucked in a deep breath and wiped her fingers under her eyes. Exhaling slowly, her gaze flicked between him and Jamie. "Don't either of you say a word." Her tone said she was holding her composure together by a thin thread.

She'd insisted that she should give Geoff's eulogy. She'd swallowed hard and often during the words she said about his life. But she'd made her way through it without breaking down, even managing a few smiles from the congregation, regaling stories of how he and her mum would run the cake stall at the village fete.

Devlin glanced over Grace's shoulder to see Mrs Cole standing together near the fireplace with Mrs Davis and Mrs Pritchett. "The weird sisters?"

She nodded. He was about to question what they said, but she preempted him by holding up a hand. "Don't ask. I saw Callum nip outside a minute ago. I might just join him for some fresh air."

Jess wandered through the living room door. "Hey. Best parties—in the hallway?"

Jamie tilted his head towards his mum. "Kitchen was full."

"More like you're worried I'll put you to work." Came the tart retort, and he blew her a kiss.

Grace grabbed her coat off the hook near the door, and Devlin helped her into it. "Do want company?" he asked quietly.

She stared up at him over her shoulder, her eyes still glistening with unshed tears. "No. I'm fine. Just a quick chat with Callum." She looked down at his leg. "You should be resting that."

His leg ached from all the sitting down and standing up during the service, and the waiting around before and after, but he wanted to be next to Grace for every moment she needed him.

"There's no way I'm sitting down with that lot of piranhas in there waiting to pounce on me and ask questions. At least standing, I can make my excuses and move away." Which was exactly how he and Jamie had ended up standing in the hallway in the first place.

Turning to face him, she gave a brief smile, rose up on her toes to kiss his cheek, and then swung around to leave by the front door.

Jess, deep in conversation with Jamie, turned and, realising Grace had left, moved to go after her. Devlin paused her with a hand on her arm. "Let her go. She'll be back in a minute."

He could see the hesitation in Jess' eyes wavering between trusting his judgement and following the best friend code. "She's not alone. Callum's out there."

She relaxed in understanding and he wondered at what point Callum had decided to follow in his father's footsteps and become the village doctor. Had he always been their confident, offering words of wisdom, or was it only since they started going to him about medical issues that he'd taken on that role?

One thing was certain, the man probably knew more than was going on in this village than he ever let on.

As Grace opened the front door, Callum turned his head to look at her. He was leaning against the dry stone wall that separated the garden from the road.

"Everything okay?" he asked.

She closed the door behind her and walked over to where he stood. "Fine. It's just a bit stifling in there."

Callum gave her a smile. "I know what you mean. I forget sometimes what it's like when there's a large village gathering. Either they're snooping into your private life, or wanting to tell you about their ailments and ask if they should make an appointment."

She shook her head in sympathy. "Every time I turn from one group to another I can hear them discussing what will happen to the house, or 'do we know what she's doing', like I wasn't still standing right there next to them."

"At least with Dad here, I can offload the older generation onto him. They still don't trust me and moan about how he was too young to retire."

They stared out across the valley for a few moments in companionable silence.

"It was a nice service. Your dad would have been pleased."

"Callum? Don't take this the wrong way, but I've had enough of talking about death for one day, maybe for a lifetime." She smiled at him to take the harshness out of her words. "Tell me more about this mystery woman I've heard Dev and Jamie talk about."

"Forget what you've heard those two say."

His words were curt. She'd obviously hit a nerve. "That you found her when you were looking for me?"

"Exactly. In fact, those two aren't supposed to be saying anything."

She placed a hand on his arm, worried about her friend. "They don't. Only between the two of them when they think I'm not listening." She didn't have to be a genius to take in Callum's rigid stance and the frown on his face to realise something was amiss. "Is she in trouble?"

Callum's lips tilted up in a grim smile. "I think more than she's telling me."

"From the way Devlin tells it, she was very lucky you found her. But I'm not sure if he's exaggerating, because it's all mixed up with him rescuing me."

"She had mild hypothermia, but if she'd lain there much longer in that storm, it would have been a different story."

"Wouldn't the army have seen her?"

Callum shrugged. "She was still on the edge of the live range, difficult to say. Certainly they've not said anything to Dev or Jamie, so I'm guessing not."

"I hope she appreciates how lucky she was."

"She does. But Grace? Someone will be looking for her once they realise she's alive. The fact that the local papers never mentioned the name of the woman who died on the moors that night is just buying her some time."

She made a gesture of zipping her lips.

"You didn't ask why I'm helping her?"

A short, sharp laugh escaped her. It felt good on such a harrowing day. "Callum, that's a given. As a little boy, you always had this gruff exterior like the whole world was against you, but if one of us was hurting, you would do everything you could to make it right." She tilted her head to study him. "We might not have had much of a chance to catch up since I returned, but from what I've seen, you haven't changed that much."

"I'm a little wiser now. Not as trusting as I once was. But she's the first person who's sparked something since that fiasco of a wedding."

Her heart ached in sympathy for him being left in the middle of a big church wedding. "I heard about that. I'm sorry."

"Perhaps it was for the best."

She nudged his shoulder with hers. "Better things can be found on the moor?"

"Maybe. We'll see."

"Well, don't leave it too long before you introduce her. You know what the gossips are like in Huntersford Leigh. If you're going to spin a story, you need to get ahead of it."

He paused as if he was considering her words before speaking again. "Did I tell you I have a friend from uni staying for a few days?"

Grace quirked an eyebrow. "No. Maybe you should come for supper one evening. Dev's bored. He could do with some company other than me."

"That would be nice."

"I'll message you and we can set something up."

The door opened behind them. She glanced over her shoulder to see Devlin's broad frame filling the doorway and swallowed hard. She still hadn't got used to the way her body reacted whenever he focused his intense gaze on her.

Since he'd come to her house last week, they'd hardly been apart. She knew it would change soon, once he was fit enough to drive into the office again, and she had some assignments coming up that would take her away, at least for a few nights.

But for now, she was enjoying every minute. Even when he grumbled about seeing if there was a workaround about the staying in the house clause, every time they slept in her single bed.

"Come on, you two," he called over. "Dad's about to make a toast."

Cal smiled and muttered underneath his breath, "This should be interesting. Mick's not knowing for holding back on what he thinks."

Grace stood where she was, horrified. Callum laughed when he saw her expression. "It's always nice, just funny observations. You'll be fine."

He took her arm and helped her back to the house. A small smile lit her lips when Dev made a point of taking her hand to pull her in through the doorway and into his embrace, leaving Cal to follow and close the door.

Maybe coming back to Huntersford Leigh wasn't going to be so bad after all.

HEART OF STONE

Thank you for visiting Huntersford Leigh!

Don't miss **Heart of Stone**—Callum and Sydney's story...

Dr Callum Stone's brusque demeanour doesn't improve when the mystery woman he rescues lies about not remembering her name but is clear on one thing—no hospital. However, his curiosity is piqued when he notices the bruises marring her skin. Injuries that look suspiciously like she's jumped from a moving car.

Sydney Carmichael is running scared. Nothing in the last twenty-four hours makes any sense, including being fired from Lois Pharmaceuticals. But Sydney knows she can't stay hidden in the idyllic village of Huntersford Leigh for long.

While she's certain beneath that stern, sexy exterior beats a heart filled with compassion, trusting Callum means exposing him to danger. Because whoever tried to silence her will return—and next time, she might not be so lucky.

ALSO BY

Huntersford Leigh
Heart of Stone
Tangled Hearts
Gathering Storm
Stealing Hearts
Chasing Lies
Ruinous Designs
Scandalous Affairs

About the Author

Sara Claridge writes contemporary romantic suspense novels that blend mystery and intrigue with passionate romance.

Born in London, her life took an unexpected turn when she followed her adventurous spirit and relocated to France several years ago on a whim. It's here, nestled in the eaves of an old farmhouse deep in the French countryside, that she lets her imagination run wild, weaving tales of love, mystery, and danger.

When not writing at her desk, Sara can often be found in the garden. Usually with a glass of red wine in one hand and a good book in the other.

For more information and to discover new releases please visit www.saraclaridge.com